SWITCHBLADE

ISSUE ELEVEN

SB

QUICK
AND
DIRTY

SHARP
AND
DEADLY

VOLUME ONE

OUTLAW CULTURE

XI

Edited by Scotch Rutherford

Switchblade, **Issue Eleven**, Volume one
First Printing: November 2019

ISBN-13: 978-1-7332976-4-6

©2019 Caledonia Press

www.switchblademag.com

Stories by the authors: © Brian Beatty, © George
Garnet © Serena Jayne, © Misha Burnett, © John
Timm, © J.D. Graves, © Alec Cizak, © Robb T. White,
© Jim Wilsky, © David Rachels

Front cover : ©2019 Scotch Rutherford
Back cover : ©2019 Scotch Rutherford

THE HUSBAND

Brian Beatty

is sitting alone

in his booth when

the diner goes dark.

the cup of coffee

in front of him almost

as cold as the snow

falling outside.

The waitress

changing clothes

back in the kitchen,

he still wants to believe,

is his wife.

All he can really

say for sure is

she's not ready yet.

Ready for what,

he doesn't know either.

The husband lights

another cigarette and

inhales, dreading their long

silent walk home

like ghosts. Or the haunted.

What if they unlock

the wrong apartment door

and collapse into

some strangers' bed?

It's happened before.

CONTENTS

EDITOR'S CORNER..3

SHARP & DEADLY SHORT FICTION

Exotic by George Garnet..............................8

Whatever Lola Wants by Misha Burnett.........20

Garden Variety Creeper by Serena Jayne....34

Strangers, Perfect Strangers by John Timm..44

Amid the Noise and Haste by J.D. Graves......59

The Radical Mr. Bogota by Alec Cizak.............78

The Alibi by Robb T. White............................88

QUICK & DIRTY FLASH FICTION

A Brand New Outfit by Jim Wilsky..............108

The Lady Urologist by David Rachels.............113

PERSON OF INTEREST..............................121

AUTHOR BIOS & ACKNOWLEGEMENTS.........131

"A GENRE-DEFYING VAMPIRE FILM"
Patrick Frater, VARIETY

"GET READY FOR THIS VAMPIRE FILM
THAT IS SURE TO LEAVE YOU JAW-DROPPED."
HORROR BUZZ

"A MODERN VAMPIRE TALE AND IT'S
NOTHING LIKE ANYTHING YOU'VE SEEN OR READ"
SWITCHBLADE
Magazine

BLOOD *from* STONE

a GEOFF RYAN *film*

starring
VANJA KAPETANOVIC · GABRIELLA TOTH · NIKA KHITROVA · ERIC COTTI

original music by GEOFF BLACK · production manager NIKA KHITROVA · hair & makeup ALETHEA SPENCER · camera ADESHOLA ADISHU · artistic director SARAH MOLISKI · grip by STEVEN VAP

executive producers LINDA NELSON · MICHAEL MADISON · GEOFF RYAN · produced by MICHAEL CARADONNA · written, directed & shot by GEOFF RYAN

INDIE
RIGHTS
MOVIES · SPORK PRODUCTIONS · ACTION CAMERA

TOUGH

CRIME STORIES

2

EDITOR'S CORNER

THIS ISSUE: DYSFUNCIONAL RELATIONSHIPS

'Relationships are everything in this business.'
Something someone I had no relationship with
once told me. People will always take whatever
you're willing to give. ☠ ☠ ☠
People you've left behind sometimes run
alongside trying to catch up. They think you
owe them a free ride. Some people think what
you've got to offer the world is something owed
to them. Then there are those peeps who
believe in an all-powerful benevolent god who
loves and protects everyone, except for those
who do not believe in him.
The strong will always feed on
the weak. And the weak will be
their feast even when they're wise,
and far more evolved. A new paint
job and a coolant flush can get
you ready for the long road ahead.
But the mileage is the killer.
People are strange,
when you're a stranger.
Get to know them,
and they become

bizarre.

—Scotch Rutherford
(Managing Editor)

FAHRENHEIT 13

AN IMPRINT OF FAHREHEIT PRESS

RISING FROM THE ASHES OF THE MUCH LOVED NUMBER
THIRTEEN PRESS - FAHRENHEIT 13 IS A NEW IMPRINT
FROM PUNK NOIR VETERANS FAHRENHEIT PRESS.

NOIR LEGEND CHRIS BLACK IS INSTALLED AS EDITOR
IN CHIEF AND IS ACCEPTING SUBMISSIONS NOW

F13NOIR@FAHRENHEIT-PRESS.COM

FAHRENHEIT 13 WILL RE-PUBLISHING ALL OF THE
ORIGINAL NUMBER THIRTEEN PRESS NOVELLAS
AS WELL AS COMMISSIONING AWESOME NEW
CRIME FICTION FROM ALL AROUND THE WORLD.

PULP ★ CRIME ★ NOIR

WWW.FAHRENHEIT-PRESS.COM

@FAHRENHEITPRESS   @F13NOIR

ECONO CLASH review # ONE

SOLDAN
McQUISTON
RUTHERFORD
MANZOLILLO
HEUNDERMANN
GRAVES
GRAY
PLATT
PERRY
NIVNER
TURNER III

QUALITY CHEAP THRILLS

EDITED BY: J.D. GRAVES

ECONO CLASH review #2 TWO

Alec Cizak
Preston Lang
Olin Wish
Robert Petyo
Victoria Dalpe
C.A. Miller
James Harper
Beatrix M.G. Nielsen
Brandon Alexander
Tom Miller
James Harper
Joshua Hill

QUALITY CHEAP THRILLS

Edited By: J.D. Graves

ECONO CLASH review #3

QUALITY CHEAP THRILLS

MAX SHERIDAN
MICHAEL BRACKEN
SARA DOBIE BAUER
RICK McQUISTON
KRISTEN BRAND
NICK SWEENEY
LEROY B. VAUGHN
BRIAN JAMES LEWIS
CHRIS STANLEY
NICOLA ZAMBANI
JOE WILLIFORD

EDITED BY: J.D. GRAVES

SPRING 2019

ECONO CLASH review #4

QUALITY CHEAP THRILLS

REX WEINER
A.B. PATTERSON
MARK SLADE
C.W. BLACKWELL
MATTHEW X. GOMEZ
JON ZELAZNY
HAILEY PIPER
J.S. ROGERS
ROBERT PETYO
J.L. BOEKESTEIN
HATEBREAKER

EDITED BY: J.D. GRAVES

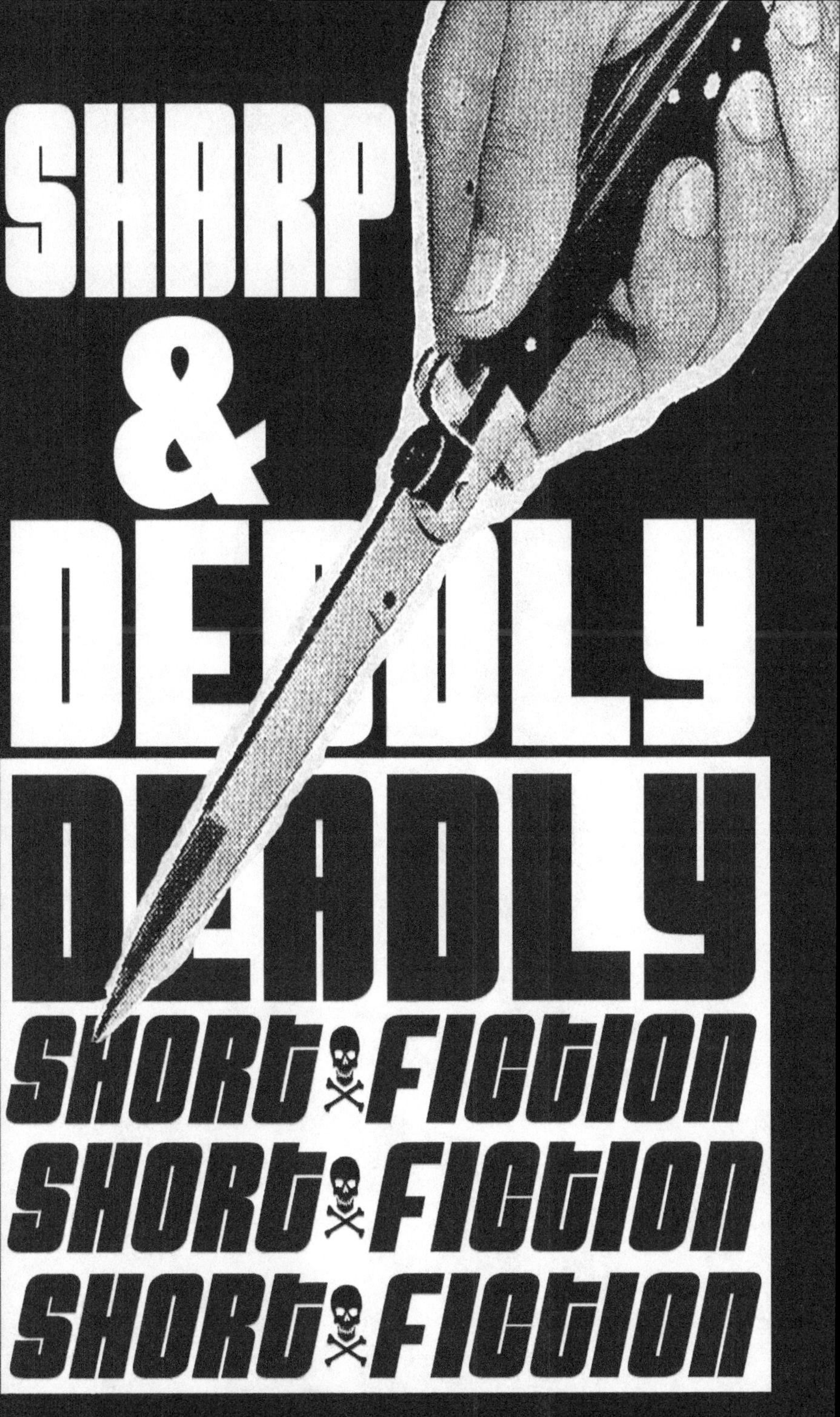

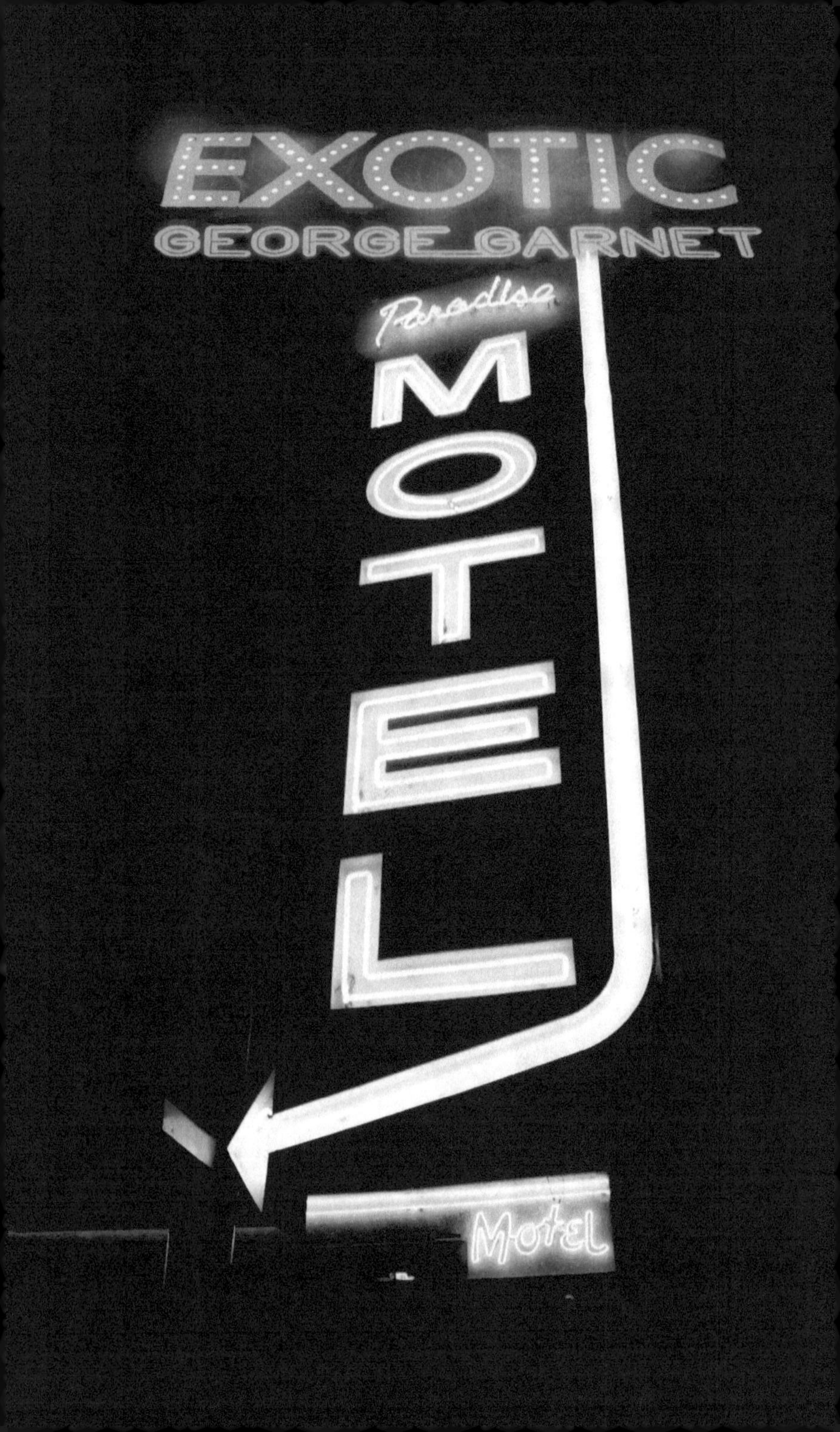
EXOTIC
GEORGE GARNET
Paradise
MOTEL
Motel

As the first drops of rain hit hard,

the man in the backseat of the silver Jaguar watches two women in miniskirts and four-inch heels across the street hurry for cover at the neon lit entrance of the old Paradise Inn.

A dozen yards away a woman in a pale yellow honey bunny short coat, red fishnets and stilettos, as if refusing to acknowledge the imminent rain doesn't run for cover, but rather takes a step towards the light pole. The halo of the streetlight morphs her into a silhouette.

"Angelo," the man flicks his fingers at the driver, a bulky man with a Borsalino hat too small for his watermelon-like head.

The driver taps the horn twice and the woman in the honey bunny stares at them for a moment before she steps off the curb and saunters across the street.

It seems she is not in a hurry. Not that desperate, huh, the man in the backseat thinks. Or too choosy, eh? He rolls the window of the Jaguar down and the cold rain, striking like pellets, stains the lapels of his perfect Armani suit.

"Hello, darling, you wanna party?" the woman speaks with an accent the man can't place. She leans forward, and the interior car lights illuminate her broad face with a straight nose and onyx eyes.

"You stainless steel?" the man says, his eyes soft like velvet.

"Huh?"

"The rain, it don't bother you?"

"The rent is too much here in Brighton Beach. You wanna party?" her accent more pronounced now.

"Haven't seen you around. You Russian?"

9

"I not do small talks unless you pay." The woman's full lips harden and she pulls back from the window.

The chubby driver jabs a meaty finger at her. "Hey, be careful how you talk to Mr.Jillie, you big mouth!"

"It's okay, Angelo," Mr. Jillie says. "Look, sweetheart, I have to ask you something. I'll pay for your time. Hop inside." He pushes the door open smoothly and pulls back making room for her.

The woman hesitates then reluctantly slides on the leather seat, her miniskirt barely reaching well shaped thighs. With delicate fingers she mops rain off her forehead. The car is warm and nice, the seat comfortable and soft, as if just made for her. She inhales a whiff of expensive men's aftershave. The car of the perfect client.

"Angelo," Mr. Jillie says and the driver turns in the front seat, unfolding an eight by ten photograph of a girl leaning against a thick cotton tree.

Mr. Jillie points with his chin at the photograph. "I bet you've seen her." The girl in the picture has thick, ebony hair, almond shaped eyes, almost melancholic. Beautiful and exotic.

"Yeah, I seen her around. Who is she?"

"One of my girls. Her name's Cora." Mr. Jillie stares at the picture for a long moment. "She's gone missing."

"I'm soo sorry to hear that." The woman swallows. "I don't know the people around here. Can't help. Sorry."

"That's okay. What's your name? Your real one?"

She glances at Mr.Jillie and her eyes slightly narrow. In this business you don't volunteer

10

anything, let alone personal information. He should know that.

Mr. Jillie puts a faint smile on his lips. "Don't matter, sweetheart. Here is the deal, you hear anything about Cora, where she might be at, or what happened to her, the corner is yours. And you will be protected by my people. Okay?" he says quietly while staring through the windshield stained by the pouring rain.

"Deal," the woman says, her eyes steady on Mr. Jillie.

"Angelo," Mr. Jillie says.

Angelo pulls out his wallet. Without a word, holding a crisp hundred-dollar bill and a business card between his two fingers, he looks at the woman.

She carefully fetches the note and the card. For a moment it's quiet, only the rain outside patters on the roof of the car. The engine of the expensive vehicle hums steadily, like a beehive.

"My name is Malina and I am not Russian," the woman says, and without waiting for an answer she reaches for the door handle.

Mr. Jillie looks at her with amusement. "Hm, not Russian. Okay." He pauses for a moment. " You might need this, Malina. It's pouring outside." He holds an old-fashioned black umbrella with a sharp metal tip. "You can have it."

She stares at Mr. Jillie, surprise in her eyes. He opens the door for her. For sure the world is full of old-fashion gentlemen that always want something from you.

Outside, the cold rain smacks her in the face, and she hastily snaps the umbrella open. The first word that comes to her mind is "fuck", which she can say in Russian, Italian, Dutch, German or English, but she prefers Bulgarian, her mother tongue. As she swears "shibania", she huddles in her short top and her high heels click on the wet concrete footpath.

The car glides away, gaining speed, its tail lights dissolving in the misty rain. She swears again and turns her back against the wind.

Despite the rain she doesn't have to wait long. A beat-up pickup stops and when the window slides down the reek of stale cigarettes and beer wafts from inside. In the light of the cabin an unshaven man mutters something while trying to focus on her.

"You need a shower, darling, not a girl. But first of all, get sober, okay?" she says tilting her head to the side. The man revs the engine in protest, spinning tires, spraying gravel, down the dark street.

Sudden wind blows cold rain in her face and she shivers.

A bit later a dark red two-seater Mazda slows, but the sirens of a speeding ambulance, scares the guy and he drives hastily away. Damn.

For a while it's quiet and she studies the shabby hotel, the narrow windows, the entrance with its half missing neon lights. The view of the grim old building stirs an unsettling feeling in her, as if she's being watched. Out of the corner of her eye she catches sight of a long black Cadillac, noiselessly pulling into the curb, just feet away from her. She always liked American cars, especially Cadillacs, but something in the way the car slide to a stop and the window roll down makes her alert. She hesitates for a second, before she steps forward.

"Hello, darling. Ready for a party?" She bends forward, holding the umbrella above her head, allowing her top to open wide. Without waiting for an answer she continues, "If you like what you see you can have it. Three fifty for the whole night." Her voice now all business.

"Slow down, sweetheart." A man's voice comes from inside the dark car. His words come slowly. Maybe he is lonely and depressed, the woman wonders.

Maybe his wife passed away not long ago and he is looking for company, a bit of warmth during the long, cold night. Maybe he just needs to talk to someone, someone to listen to his story. She knows everything about those feelings and that's why she makes herself sound a bit desperate too. This is her strategy - looking too eager to make the sale, men usually take her for a newbie, something a lot of johns prefer. Often innocence is more attractive than the seasoned, emotionally devoid street escort. Briefly she wonders why they call them 'johns'.

"Okay," the woman says in her Bulgarian English, and smiles.

"Do I hear an accent? Where are you from?"

"I live in Brighton Beach, but originally I am from Bulgaria. "Following her strategy, she tells the truth. The man is in the bag. And that about Bulgaria, most of the times this is seen like an advantage. An exotic woman. Americans usually have never heard of Bulgaria. Once she told a client that Bulgaria was in central Africa and they bought it.

"That's very nice, sweetheart. Haven't met any girl from Bulgaria yet. Isn't that the sixteenth republic of Russia?" The car interior lights suddenly come alive. A man, likely in his 60s - grey short hair, narrow clean shaven face, sagging cheeks - stares at her with unblinking eyes.

"You know too much, honey." She laughs, looking approvingly at his white shirt and dark blue navy suit. Clean. She pauses and shivers theatrically."It's cold and wet outside."

"Sure, sure, sweetheart." The man opens the passenger door.

"Thank you, darling." The woman folds the umbrella and takes her time getting inside. She sinks into the comfortable leather seat and leans back. The car is clean and the fragrance of fresh pine floats inside. She relaxes and while she is placing the wet umbrella at her feet, the cold, unblinking eyes of her companion slide down her chest, her flat tummy, down her well shaped thighs.

"My place, sweetheart?" the man says.

"Is it far away? I have a room at the Lemon Grass."

"Better my place, it's just three blocks down. What's your name, sweetheart?"

"Malina," she says and smiles. "Meaning Raspberry in English."

"How romantic." The man marvels, his cold eyes focused on her glossy, slightly parted, full lips.

Three blocks later they stop in front of a small one-story house with almost no front yard, big old oaks towering from both sides of the narrow road. The neighborhood is dark and quiet. The rain, now a drizzle, rustles in the yellow leaves of the oaks. A corner lamp casts a dim cone of light on the deserted street.

The man, with unusual lightness for his age, jogs on the broken path to the house followed by the woman, her high heels sinking in the wet footpath. He unlocks the house and flips a switch, an old chandelier casting a dim, yellowish light in a long narrow corridor. He holds the door open for her.

"Here we are." The man's thin lips stretch in a cold smile.

A musty smell wafting from inside, makes her think about mothballs and she holds her breath for a moment. She wonders if this is really the place where the man lives. However since she has been doing this job nothing surprises her.

"The first door to the right." He points down the corridor.

While she is folding the umbrella he watches her from behind. She looks perfect. He feels a tingling in his loins. He's never had a Bulgarian woman: great looking, with a healthy body and a sweet Bulgarian accent. Such a catch. If he knew he could've learned more about Bulgaria beforehand. It's always enticing to know more about your future belongings. Like the one from Madeira and especially the last girl, from Belize. Until the last second she had given him such pleasure. But that was last month. Definitely tonight will be something exceptional, something much better.

He trembles with excitement, his heart pumping strong. He's feeling younger, ready for the adrenaline rush that is coming. Shaken, he steadies himself. No, he can't wait that long. He drops the house key in his jacket pocket.

Followed by the man, she enters the first room to the right. It's a bedroom with an old fashioned double bed, covered with an afghan, a small desk in the corner and a wooden chair. Too bare, the floor just linoleum.

The man, behind her, steps close and gently snakes his arms around her. She smells his perfume and inhales. Nautica. Fresh and ambient like a blue sea. The man's cheeks are soft, well shaven. She likes this. She likes men who look after themselves. It shows self respect and self worth.

He sniffs her hair, his lips tracing her left ear. His hands move smoothly down the swell of her breasts, feeling them. Firm. They don't seem to be fake. He has a lot of experience detecting fakes. These are real, their shape perfect, the nipples slightly above the swell. He feels them, gently. The nipples harden like rubies.

She moans. She likes soft, clean, slow hands. She doesn't mind the age. Sometimes older men are fun, much more balanced than the young guys who have only one thing in mind - pushing and gorging. Like bulls. What kind of fun is that?

His fingers unbutton her top and he lightly pulls back, taking it off. Then he slides his lips just below her ear, down her neck, the beautiful area, her skin tight and smooth, the skin of a young woman, firm like an apple, waiting to be bitten and swallowed...

Realising that she is still holding the folded umbrella, she leans forward to place it behind the door when something slips around her neck and yanks her back.

Startled, she grabs for the thing around her neck, her nails scraping her own skin. The thing sinks into her flesh, her eyes bulging. Gasping for air, she tries in vain to inhale, her chest bursting. As her hands punch the air, her fingers grab on to something. The umbrella. Like a drowning person grasping a straw she clutches hard, one hand on the handle, the other squeezing the umbrella's stem. Fight if you have been surprised by an attacker! She recalls from the week-long course for exotic dancers she took, before leaving Bulgaria. Face the attacker and hit hard.

In a desperate move she twists, and with a powerful swing she drives the sharp umbrella tip into something behind her. It's the man's thigh. He growls with pain and loosens his grip on the Capron rope. The woman inhales with a gasp and a surge of oxygen rushes into her lungs, delivering fresh energy to her muscles. With new found strength she kicks the wall in front and her assailant, propelled by the force, loses balance and topples on his back to the floor. With the agility of a cat, the woman jumps to her feet. Holding the umbrella like a spear she thrusts it at the man's chest. His wallet, tucked in his breast pocket, cushions the blow. "Stop, stop!" he grunts.

The woman swears, "Shiban idiot" and shoves her knee in his chest hard. Blood gushing from his thigh stains her legs.

"Stop, please stop..." he keeps squealing.

"You sick fuck!" She is ready to drive the metal umbrella tip into his throat but restrains herself. She breaths in and out a few times to subdue the adrenalin rush. "Killer! Fucking killer!" Her face a contorted mask. "Where are the other women?" Slowly she leans forward applying pressure on the umbrella, the sharp metal tip just piercing the man's sagging throat skin. "Precisely where did you bury them?"

He winces but says nothing.

"Where?" She curses, "Shiban pervert!"

The man clenches his teeth, his eyes glassy now. No, he won't talk.

She looks into those lifeless, wide open eyes. Ice cold. She keeps peering in there, hypnotized, drawing some dark energy from a deep black well. Contagious. Slowly, she pulls the umbrella back, her knee squeezing the man's chest.

"Have you heard of the Bulgarian umbrella? Maybe you read about it in the newspapers, years ago. The Bulgarian secret service had to silence an enemy living in London. They didn't send a sniper. They just sent a man with an umbrella." She pauses to let him contemplate the sleek black object. "As a fighting stick, it is a good weapon. As a rifle, it is deadly. It shoots poison pellets. Ricin. An agonising slow death."

The woman points the metal tip at the man's throat, an inch away. The snake eyes blink a few times and his Adam's apple moves up and down rapidly.

"I... I buried them under the Fisherman's bridge down the river." His trembling voice a whisper.

"How many?" She touches the umbrella's tip to his throat.

"Two."

She kicks him hard. In one of the table drawers she finds duct tape. "I bet this was for me," she says while taping his hands and legs.

"One last thing, you creep. Bulgaria has never been the 16th state of Russia!"

She fishes out his phone from his jacket and dials the number.

*

"Both corpses?" Mr. Jillie talks into his cell phone while standing, his Armani suit immaculate.

He listens, before he continues, "Okay, the description of one of the bodies matches her clothes. It's Cora." He ends the call and thoughtfully pockets the cell phone. The bodies of two missing escorts found. He sighs. Cora was a

18

good escort, a lot of johns liked her. She wasn't supposed to die this way. Her killer, the psychopath, tightly wrapped in thick plastic by Angelo is already stuffed in the boot of an old Ford outside, one that will be torched later.

Mr. Jillie shakes a wrinkle off his sleeve and looks at Malina sitting on the only chair in the room. "You okay?" he says.

"I am fine."

"I'll cover your fee and any extra work for tonight. I'm sorry about the mess."

"Yeah." She blinks, her eyelids heavy. "You'll keep your word about the corner spot?"

"Sure. We had a deal." He pauses and cups his jaw. "Just one last thing. How did you get him talking?"

She gets up slowly from the chair. "Was easy. Like a walk in park as you Americans say. He was very talkative man."

Mr Gillie taps his front teeth with his finger.

She takes a step towards him, her eyes tired. "Look, it's been a long day. I need a shower, breakfast and bed. Maybe another time. Oukay?"

"Just curious."

She reaches for the umbrella on the table, slides her palm over the silk-smooth fabric, and hands it to him.

"It's a Bulgarian secret." Her lips stretch in a faint smile and before he opens his mouth she is already at the door.

"A Bulgarian secret?" Mr. Jillie echoes her words while staring at the door closing behind her.

***

WHATEVER
LOLA WANTS

HARVEST
INN

MOTEL

MISHA
BURNETT

My wife and I once had sex in the shower stall of a stranger's

apartment while a party was going on outside the bathroom. We had been married for six months and had already found ourselves drifting away from the old crowd, isolated by the sense that we had done something irrevocably adult. The party had been thrown by some friend of a friend and we both found it dull and quite suddenly she took me by the hand and led me down the hallway and there in the bathroom she backed me up against the wall and unzipped my pants.

We leaned against the wall and she was shockingly wet, her hands gripping me and I was hard and inside her before I could quite believe that she was doing this, surrounded by stained green tile, her grin speaking silent volumes and it was over so quick but she didn't mind, just rearranged her clothes and led me out again.

We left shortly after that and we never spoke of it, but sometimes I would catch her eye and be certain that she was thinking of that moment and her sudden and absolute conquest of me.

Some mornings I wake up in my bed, that used to be our bed, and I see her twisted between the rails of her own bed and before I am fully awake and beginning the day's chores I remember that moment and I think of what I would give to have that again, just one last time.

But this is how we live now.

I wake up before the alarm, every day, and I slip out of my bed to make coffee and light the day's first cigarette. I have few precious minutes, maybe as long as a half hour, to organize the day in my mind. On weekdays I make us some breakfast before I go off to work. While I'm in the kitchen I hear her waking and getting out of bed. I stay in the kitchen, even though I hate to hear her struggling and I want to help her.

She doesn't want me to help, though, not with that. She's told me that she has to be able to transfer from her bed to her chair by herself, she has to know that she can do that much. As long as she can get to the chair she's not helpless.

I respect that. I listen hard, in case she really does need me and calls my name, but I let her do that by herself.

She rolls out and we have breakfast together. I wash the dishes and put them away while she rolls into the living room to log into her computer for the day. She does medical billing, working remotely, and it doesn't pay much but the hospital has good health benefits. We need those.

Then I go off to work. I sell plumbing fittings, wholesale. I used to be a plumber, back before my wife's accident, so I know my product line. I don't make as much with this job, but I don't have to go out at night any more. I don't like leaving her alone after dark.

Sometimes I do go out, though, in the evenings, for a couple of hours. I'll go out to a bar, have a few drinks. My wife tells me to go out and have a good time, that she'll be fine.

It was a Wednesday in April, one of those raw cold days that feels like a flashback to February, and I was leaving work for lunch when I saw the kid leaning against my car. He was skinny, in a ratty coat too big for him. I figured he was waiting for the bus and I was about to ask him politely to move along, when he gave me a big grin.

"Hey, honey," he said. "Miss me?"

I frowned at him, trying to place his face.

His smile was replaced by a theatrical pout. "You don't recognize me, do you?"

And then I did. I'd never seen him dressed as a man before.

"Hi, Lola," I said. "It's been a while."

"Ninety days," he said. "Shoplifting."

"You were in jail?" I asked. I did not like him hanging around my car. I wasn't even sure how he'd found out where I worked.

"Total bullshit," he said. "I didn't do a damn thing. But the idiot PD they gave me told me to plead."

"What are you doing here?" I asked pointedly.

"You know it's cold as shit out here, right?" he shot back. "You wanna maybe get in the car? We could go get a burger or something. You know, for old times sake?"

"Why are you here?" I repeated, making no move to my car.

He leaned forward. "What's the problem, honey? Scared your buddies might see you with me?"

"I just want to know your business," I said, not wanting to admit how right he was.

I had met him—as Lola—on one of my nights out. We had worked out an arrangement. A strictly business arrangement. I wasn't proud of it, and I had been relieved and disappointed in equal measure when he'd dropped out of sight.

He dropped his voice into the husky whisper he'd used as Lola. "Maybe I just want to suck that fat cock of yours one more time."

"Get out of here," I told him, keeping my voice down with effort. "We're done."

He laughed then, a faggy falsetto laugh. "Or maybe I want to go home with you and meet the wife. We could have such a nice talk, her and I. Girl talk, you know?"

I took a step towards him and my hands made fists before I could stop them. "You leave her out of this."

"Or what?" he asked. "You gonna get all manly and kick my ass? You big butch bruiser, you."

I took a deep breath. "Just tell me what you want."

"I want to get out of this fucking wind," he said. "Come on, man, let's go get a burger. We can talk in the car."

I clicked the fob to unlock the doors. I knew I was making a mistake when I did it, but I gestured for him to get in.

As I pulled out of the lot and turned on the heater he said, "Hey, got a cigarette?"

I handed over my pack. There was a drive-thru a couple of blocks away, and headed that direction.

"My cheerleader uniform got ruined," Lola said in a plume of smoke. "When I got sent up this fat-ass queen where I was staying decided to go through my shit and ripped the seams trying to stuff into it. Can you believe that shit? And my silver wig is gone. Just gone. Faggots, man, they'll steal anything."

"You got a new place to stay?" I asked. I didn't care, I was just trying to make conversation.

"Yeah, I'm at this lame halfway house. All kinds of rules in that place. I got to get a straight job so they'll let me move out," he said.

Despite myself I had a sudden and uncomfortably vivid memory of his mouth on me. When dressed up Lola didn't look like a woman, not exactly, he was too exaggerated, too much a caricature. His face was painted almost clown-like, eyelashes a half inch long, powdered cheeks, lips painted fire engine red. I remembered him on his knees, applying lipstick before he... did what I paid him for.

"Is that what you need?" I asked. "A job?"

"I need to get my life together, man," He stubbed out his cigarette and lit another from my pack. "I don't want to end up like those old queens, turning tricks in bus station toilets. I'm off the weed, I'm gonna get my GED. I just need, you know, a little hand up."

"You can use me as a reference," I said. "to get a job."

We reached the drive-thru and I ordered us two meals. I didn't bother asking him for money for his, I just paid for both.

He attacked his burger and fries like he thought I'd take it away from him of he didn't eat it fast enough. I pulled into a spot at the back of the lot and ate mine a little more leisurely.

He wiped ketchup off his lips with his thumb and again I remembered his mouth. I looked out the window.

"I can ask around," I offered. "See if anyone is hiring."

"I got a gig lined up," he said. "This guy I met inside offered me a job. Installing vinyl floors. You know that stuff that looks like wood, but it's really just plastic strips? He pays by the job, and I could make decent money."

"That sounds good." I finished up my burger and wadded up the paper. I hadn't turned off the car, so I just put it in reverse and pulled out.

"You gonna eat your fries?" he asked.

I handed them over.

"The thing is," he said, mouth full, "I need six hundred bucks. Like, for tools and this class and shit."

"Oh." I should have seen it coming.

"So I was thinking maybe you could loan me the money and I'll pay you back once I'm working," he said, his tone deliberately casual, like six hundred dollars was no big deal.

26

"I haven't got that kind of money," I said bluntly. "I sell faucets, okay? My wife is paralyzed. We're just barely scraping by."

"I could be really nice to you." In Lola's voice. I hated myself for the thrill that sent down my spine.

We were back at the warehouse. I slammed my car into a parking space. By the dashboard clock my lunch was over in four minutes.

"I haven't got it," I said.

He looked at me.

"So get it," he smiled at me. "Or I have a chat with your wife."

There was something cold and primal in his eyes, something I had never seen before.

I had known Lola was a mask, a false face he'd put on to fool the world into thinking he was something alluring and harmless, but I saw now that the scrawny kid whom I'd seen leaning on my car was a mask, too. I caught a glimpse of the predator underneath all the masks, the real man behind the lipstick and powder.

It scared me.

"Think about it, okay?" he said. "I'll be in touch."

And he was out the door.

I made it back inside in time, but just barely.

When I got home that night my wife apologized for not having dinner ready, Her hips had been bothering her and she hadn't felt up to it. I told her not to worry about it and started some ground turkey browning on the stove.

"Is something wrong?" my wife asked.

"Just work," I told her. "Nothing important."

Lola let me stew for five days.

Over the weekend I took my wife to the mall, pushing her chair through the weekend crowds to the multiplex where we saw some movie I don't remember at all and after that to dinner that was pricier than I was comfortable with. I smiled, though, and I did what I could to make her happy. That was what was important, making her happy.

No matter what it cost.

On Monday Lola was back, leaning on my car again at lunch time. This day was warm, spring having returned with a vengeance. He was in a sleeveless T-shirt and skinny jeans.

"Well?" he asked airily, "Can you help me or do I go talk to the missus?"

"I can help you," I said, "But I want you to do something for me."

"Sure, honey," he smiled. His lips weren't as pretty without paint. "Anything you like."

"I want the usual, and I want Lola," I said. I lowered my voice. "Understand? I want you to be my girl. You still got your red dress, or did they take that, too?"

"I still got my red dress," he purred, "and for six hundred you get the royal treatment. When do you want it?"

"Tomorrow night," I said. "After work. Six o'clock at the Harvest Inn. I'll meet you in the bar. This is the last time. After this, we're done."

"If that's the way you feel about it, baby." he said in Lola's voice.

My wife had dinner ready when I got home, lasagna and peas, both microwaved. I told her that I was going out with friends from work the next evening, and that I wouldn't be home for dinner.

She agreed to that easily, as I knew she would, and suggested going for a drive that weekend, and seeing some local wineries. We hadn't done that since her accident, but she said that she'd checked on-line and had a list of places that said they were wheelchair accessible. The weather was supposed to be beautiful.

I told her that it sounded like fun, and she smiled like Christmas morning.

I had problems sleeping that night.

Lola. I didn't even know his real goddamned name. He'd been named that by some older queen. He hadn't even known about the Kinks song until I told him. Increasingly though, it hadn't been Ray Davies I had heard when I thought that name, but Gwen Verdon's song in *Damn Yankees*.

"Whatever Lola wants
Lola gets..."

I had never tried to pretend that I thought he was a real girl. He never tried to pass, not seriously. He was a walking pinup, a parody of a woman, a pose that concealed—not very convincingly—a contempt for actual females.

29

It was that artifice that I had found irresistible. It was like... it was like I wasn't cheating, because Lola wasn't a real person. In fishnets and paint and ridiculous falsies he'd made himself into a cartoon.

The only part of him that was real was the hot wet cavern of his mouth. I'd look down past the wig and eyelashes and lipstick to where I was entering that mouth.

"You can't get that from your wife," he always say, afterwards, not knowing how true, in my case, that was. I'd never told him anything personal about myself, but somehow he'd found out where I worked, and probably where I lived.

Even if I'd had six hundred dollars to give him, I knew it wouldn't stop there. Once he knew I'd pay, he'd find something else to ask me for, some other "loan". I had to stop him, and I had to stop him now.

Make up your mind to have no regrets, I told myself, and at last I was able to sleep.

The next day I was in the bar at the Harvest Inn, at a back corner table, by five-thirty, nursing a beer. Lola came in at ten minutes after six, making a splash as he always did. He really had pulled out all the stops tonight, a blonde wig that looked new, the red dress I remembered, bodice bulging with stuffing, high heeled boots, fishnets.

Everybody stared as he made his way across the bar to my table.

Good. They were staring at him. Nobody was going to be able to remember what I looked like.

30

"Don't sit down," I said softly. "Room sixteen. Head on down there, I'll follow you in a minute."

The painted face pouted. "Oh, are you shy?" He extended a red-nailed hand. "I need the key."

I shook my head. "It's open."

It would be, too. I'd taped the latch after I climbed in through the window. Rooms at the Harvest Inn had doors that opened into the parking lot, not an internal hallway. Number sixteen was at the far end of the lot, and there weren't any cars parked close to it.

Hotel records would show that room as vacant, and the only camera in the whole place was in the lobby, over the cash register. I hadn't been near the lobby.

I gave Lola ten minutes by the clock over the bar. I finished my beer and left the empty glass and a dollar tip on the table. On the way across the lot I pulled on my gloves. Mechanics gloves, heavy and waterproof.

He was sitting on the bed when I walked in, demurely, knees together and skirt pulled down. The drapes were closed and the only light was from the bathroom.

I closed the door behind me and took two steps, half crossing the tiny room.

"Got my money?" He asked in his Lola voice.

"You first," I said. "You know what I want."

He slid gracefully off the bed and onto his knees. "You got a lollipop for Lola?"

As his red nails touched my fly I reached up for the pipe I'd laid on top of the TV when I'd broken into the room.

Three quarter inch black iron by thirteen inches long. A piece of scrap left over from a customer's custom cut order. No one would miss it, and there was no way to trace it back to me.

Lola never had the chance to scream. My first blow knocked his blonde wig off and tumbled him against the bed. I hit him again on the side of the head, and he fell limp as a rag doll.

I followed him down to the floor and made sure of the job. My first blows had the strength of fear and rage behind them. Now I worked methodically, like I hammering an inlet valve free of a rusted-out boiler. His head was pulp when I was done. There was no movement in his chest, no pulse in his wrists.

No more Lola.

I shoved the body under the bed and tossed the pipe in after it. In the bathroom mirror I checked myself and washed the blood off, then wiped the sink clean.

There was a wet stain by the foot of the bed, but it would dry and the carpet was one of those splotchy brown and green patterns designed to hide stains. With luck it would be days before someone rented this room and found the body.

On the way home I changed my shirt and threw my gloves and shirt away in a dumpster behind a Chinese restaurant.

That weekend I took my wife on a long drive through the country. We found a winery up on the bluffs that could accommodate her chair and took the tour. She had some samples and got flushed, her eyes shining like they used to, so long ago.

They had outside seating for lunch and we sat together on a deck high above the river, in the sunlight and the open air.

She reached across and took my hand. "Thank you," she said, "this is lovely."

"Anything for you," I told her.

And I meant it.

***

GARDEN VARIETY CREEPER

SERENA JAYNE

On Saturday afternoon, the doorbell rang. Instead of the big box of books she'd ordered, Jane found Harry standing on her porch. His hairline had retreated another half-inch or so, and he wasn't wearing the lifts in his shoes that brought him up to her height of five feet, six inches. In short, he looked just as humdrum as he had when they'd worked together doing data entry at Sterling and Graves five years earlier.

The stranger-danger alarm in her head buzzed. A false alarm. Harry was neither a stranger nor a danger.

"May I come in?" He shoved his hairy hands deep inside the pockets of his baggy beige pants. A small strip of duct tape shone from the hem of his winter coat. With his double chin and mournful basset hound brown eyes, he looked as benign as the pencil eraser-sized mole on his forehead.

She opened the door wide, and he stepped inside.

"Would you like something to drink?" She cursed her mother's insistence on manners.

"Some good old H2O would be much appreciated."

She led the way to the kitchen and filled a glass from the pitcher of water she kept in the refrigerator. "The ice machine is busted. Sorry."

He took the glass and their fingers brushed.

The spider-silk sensation of the touch made her shiver. She wiped her hands on her jeans.

Instead of taking a seat at the tiny table, he stood so close she could smell his sour breath. The room seemed to shrink to the dimensions of a closet packed with winter coats and boots.

"How are…" She faltered trying to recall his wife's name. "Mindy and the kids?"

"Lindy's fine. She's obsessed with her book club." He took a sip of water and his Adam's apple bobbed. "We have three boys now. Junior is ten, Henry is six, and Horace hits the nine-month mark next week."

The heavy musk of his aftershave made her throat constrict.

"What brings you to the city?"

"When the Christmas card I'd sent you came back, I thought you'd moved again. Then I realized there wasn't a sticker with your new address. The post office can be oh so helpful."

She picked at her cuticles and bit her lip. Her friends had convinced her that getting unsettled by something so insignificant was silly. Tired of hearing her complain, they had suggested letting Harry know his cards were unwelcome.

She could have called him. After all, he faithfully scribbled his phone number inside every card, but the idea of talking to him made her stomach ache. Instead of sticking the latest card into the shredder as usual, she'd written 'return to sender' in big, bold letters and dropped it in the mail.

Now here he was, live and in person, standing in her kitchen, and the request to stop sending cards remained jammed in her throat.

"Sterling and Graves sure lost out when you quit. No one does Secret Santa as well as you do. Every year someone mentions how you covered the director's office with candy canes and fake snow." He wiped his mouth on his sleeve. "How do you like working at the Hawthorne Company?"

36

"It's okay." She wasn't about to mention that she recently revamped her resume after an incident with a contractor at a work event. The sleaze-ball had snapped a photo of her, cropped it down to just her breasts, and made the picture his phone screen image.

Even though she was fully clothed in modest business casual attire, his actions made her feel dirty. She'd tossed the floral blouse into the trash the minute she'd gotten home. Despite filing a harassment complaint with Human Resources, the contractor remained assigned to the project.

"Where's your bathroom?" Harry set the glass in the sink.

"Down the hall, first door on the right."

"Great, thanks." He shuffled away.

She scrubbed at the glass with a soapy sponge. Soon he'd be gone, and she could forget about him until the next holiday. Harry sent her cards for St. Patrick's Day, Labor Day, Arbor Day, Sweetest Day, Halloween, as well as for her birthday.

She'd asked around. He didn't send greeting cards to other past or present employees of Sterling and Graves. And she'd never told him her birthday or given him her address.

Twenty minutes passed and Harry hadn't returned. Jane couldn't bear the thought of him dying of a heart attack while sitting on her toilet, but what she discovered was much worse.

She found Harry in her bedroom. One hairy wrist was fastened to her bedframe with handcuffs lined with magenta fur. The vibrant color contrasted with his pasty skin tone. He was naked but for his triumphant smile.

Her mouth went dry and her heart pounded. "What? Why?"

"I've always liked you, Jane. Sure, you're dumpy and you've got a butter-face, but those big tits and ass of yours are something special."

A hot flush crawled up her neck and her hands shook. "Get out, or I'm calling the police."

"Don't bother. You let me inside your apartment. If I tell them you seduced me, who are they going to believe? The guy with the wife and three kids or some single slut?"

She remembered the look the Human Resources Manager gave her when she'd reported the contractor. The look that said he didn't believe her. The look that said men didn't bother with women like her when there were better specimens to ogle.

Even if she had kept them, she'd be hard-pressed to get a police officer to consider the cards harassment. In her worst nightmares, she'd never expected to see Harry again, let alone shackled to her bed. Spread out like a starfish from hell on her flowered comforter.

"You owe me, Jane. I've spent money and time on you. It's time for a little quid pro quo."

Harry's patience was legendary. Many times at Sterling and Graves, the management had conceded to his silly suggestions, because he refused to back down.

"What do you want from me?" Her voice was screechy with panic.

"Lindy thinks blow jobs are dirty and disgusting. I'll leave, but only after you put that mouth of yours to work on me." He snacked his lips.

Jane gagged. Grabbing her purse, she fled and locked herself in the bathroom.

"I'm not going anywhere until you do your duty. I've got all the time in the world." Harry's baritone voice seemed to slither through the space under the door.

Clutching her purse to her chest, she sank down to the cold ceramic tile, and wracked her brain trying to think of someone who could help. Someone who'd believe her. Her best friend might listen, but she didn't want to put another woman at risk.

She was tired of men who expected her to feel grateful for whatever unwelcome attention they sent her way. She couldn't help but think of the dude at the gym who always made a point to set up his yoga mat directly behind hers. While attempting to massage her shoulders, the man told her she turned the workout into "hot yoga."

Despite changing her attire from sports bras and form-fitting leggings to baggy shirts and sweatpants, he kept attempting to touch her.

The day he'd followed her to the parking lot and kept insisting she let him buy her a smoothie, she'd quit yoga for good, and she'd taken to carrying a weapon. One that sat like a deadly metal lump at the bottom of her purse.

Harry was a reptile. She'd assumed he was the garter snake of guys, not a rattler or a cobra or a boa constrictor, but she'd been wrong. Not all monsters looked scary, and that made them even more dangerous.

Setting her jaw, she stripped down to her underwear. She slipped her hand around the cold metal at the bottom of her handbag.

"I'll come out if you agree to my conditions," she called. "You must stay cuffed. I'll touch you, but you can't touch me."

"Strip club rules. I can work with that." The bedsprings creaked. "I'm ready and waiting. Let's play, Plain Jane."

Her heart slamming in her chest, she unlocked the door and stepped into the bedroom.

Harry rattled his handcuff. "For your birthday, I'm going to buy you sexier lingerie. Your bra and panties are made for function rather than fun."

She resisted the urge to tug on her sports bra and boy shorts to ensure maximum coverage. "Let's not get ahead of ourselves. Close your eyes."

"Since it's our first time, you can call the shots. Next time I'll be the one in charge." His eyelids fluttered shut.

After using her phone to snap a photo, she slid the cold metal of the brass knuckles onto her dominant hand and curled her fingers into a fist.

Adrenaline zipped along her veins. She hid her hand behind her back and took a step forward.

Harry opened his eyes. "Don't be a tease. Get over here and give me what I deserve."

"That I can do." She climbed onto the bed and straddled him, pinning his free arm with her knee.

Bile rose in her throat.

"That's more like it. Now, be a good little stripper, and lose the rest of your clothes."

"First things first." She drew back and punched him in the collarbone.

A snap sounded.

He let out an unholy howl and bucked. Kicking and scratching and flailing.

She got in a blow to his midsection before he unseated her, and she tumbled to the ground. Pain pounding from various places, she stumbled to her feet.

"You crazy bitch." His eyes were wide, and his breathing ragged. "I need a doctor." He made a grab for her wrist.

She delivered a whack to his knee.

He shrieked.

"No cards. No presents. No visits. Got it? We're not friends or acquaintances." She shook her fist in the direction of his crotch. "If I ever see you again, I'll make for damned sure you don't have a fourth child."

He worked to unfasten the cuffs and his face went gray. "Okay, you win. I'll leave." Snot dripped from his nose and tears glittered in his eyes.

For a split second, Jane worried that by beating Harry senseless, she'd become the monster. She shook the thought from her mind. Had Harry not crossed the line from friendly to fiendish, she'd never have hurt him.

With slow robotic movements, he gathered his clothes and shrugged on his coat.

As soon as he was gone, she locked the front door behind him and returned to the bedroom. Her head buzzed, and her arm ached.

One of Harry's sweat socks peaked out from under the bed. In a corner, a pair of gray boxer briefs with a worn out elastic band sat abandoned. Blood dotted the comforter and the old pair of brass knuckles.

Thanks, Gramps. When she was a teenager, he'd presented her with the weapon. At the time, she'd wished he'd given her money for a video game, but she'd enjoyed using the brass knuckles to hit bales of hay in his barn. Gramps would be proud to know his gift helped her protect herself.

She'd take a shower and eradicate all evidence of Harry, but it wouldn't change the fact that he'd violated the sanctuary of her home.

*

41

Three months passed without a peep from Harry. One of Jane's friends at Sterling and Graves mentioned that Harry blamed his injuries on a mugging.

While the other book club were oohing and ahhing over the assortment of confectionaries she'd brought to the community center, Jane slid a small envelope inside the pages of the book she'd lifted from the hostess's chair.

She nodded to the woman who'd returned to reclaim her book and her seat. "Great choice this month, Mindy. Some Hollywood bigwig just snapped up the film rights."

"It's Lindy." The woman plucked the envelope from the pages and her forehead scrunched up.

Jane sipped her coffee.

The other book club members chatted with each other, waiting for their leader to open the discussion about the latest selection.

Lindy gaped at the sympathy card and the glossy photo of Harry. She yelped and slapped the book over the damning evidence that showed her husband in all his sleazy glory. Her face broke out in red splotches, and her lower lip trembled.

Jane hated making Lindy collateral damage, but she needed to break the cycle.

The message inside was simple. Don't let Horace and Henry and Harold Junior become creepers like their dear old dad. In case Lindy had any questions, Jane had kindly scrawled the phone number of her brand new burner phone inside.

Harry had violated her home and damaged her dignity, but Jane had found her voice. Next time a creeper came calling, she'd inform them that their suggestive comments and advances were unwanted. If all else failed, she had Gramps's brass knuckles and the courage to use them.

***

©2019 Serena Jayne

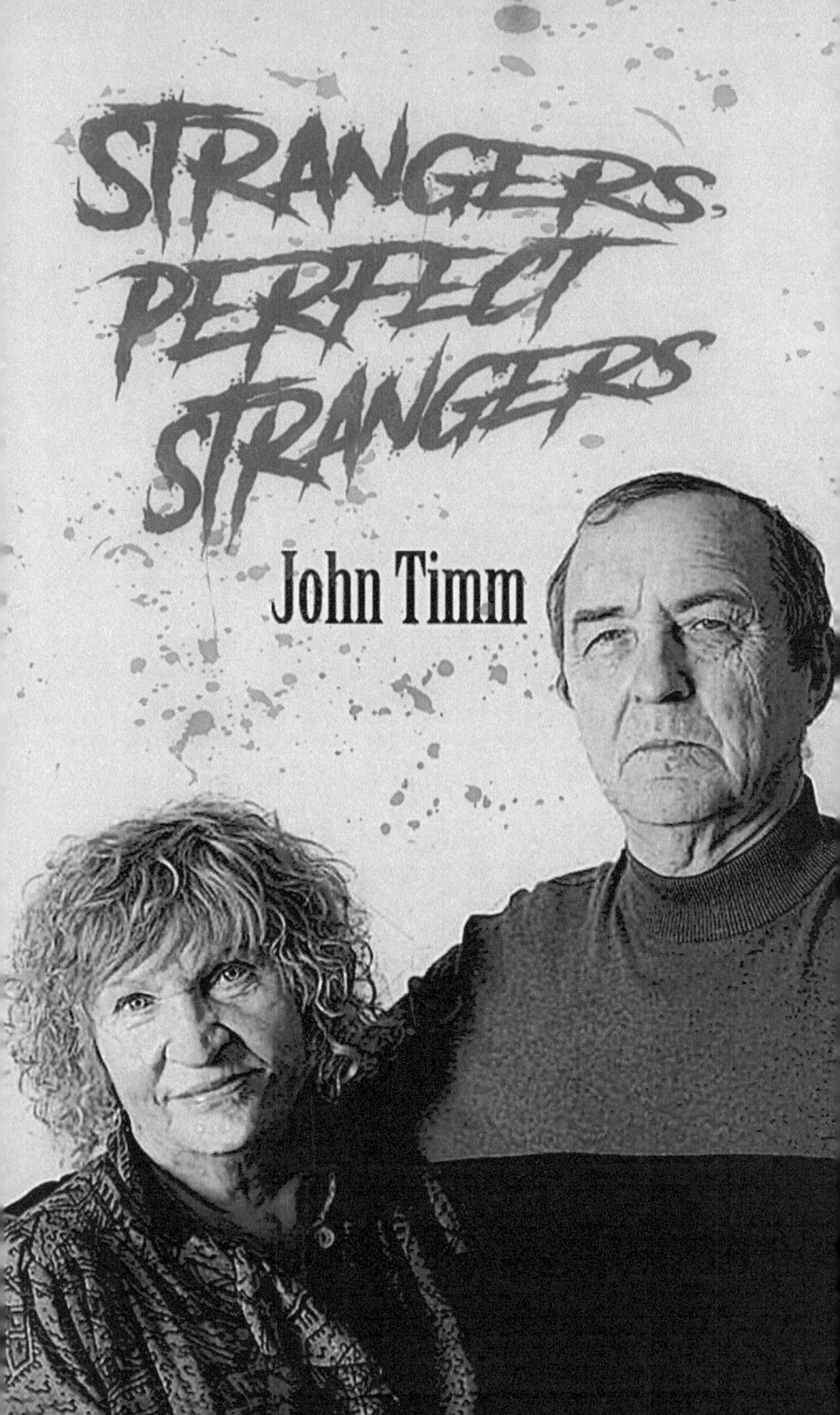

STRANGERS, PERFECT STRANGERS

John Timm

To say Vince Long had misgivings about marrying Haley Prentiss would be a gross understatement. Yes, he was in love with her— at least up to a point. And yes, he constantly daydreamed of a life of unaccustomed wealth, with the cars, the houses, the travel, the status he had never known until he met Haley, until he had unleashed that special charm of his upon her. But he was young, with plently of rich, pretty girls still out there, still waiting to be charmed. For Vince Long, leaving the hedonistic joys of the single life behind would be difficult at best.

Vince knew he was a charmer, and he'd made the most of it ever since high school, through college, and on into his twenties in his current role as junior financial advisor for a major brokerage firm. So despite their engagement, there still existed that urge to "explore more options," as he liked to call it—only to himself, of course. All the while, there was the ever loyal Haley, standing by until he graduated, until he found his first job, until he got "better situated."

The emotions had been equally mixed on the part of Haley's family. Strong opposition at first—after all, he hardly fit the mold of the young men Haley was accustomed to dating. And there was nothing in his working class background to recommend him socially. But Vince's charisma and street smarts had mostly won them over, now that the wedding date was set. With great reluctance, her father's attorney even dropped his recommendation of a prenuptial agreement. Haley had insisted, "He'll soon be making so much in the market, my money will be of little matter." Her protest didn't sit well with her father, either, but in the end, his daughter, his only daughter, always got what she wanted. Always.

*

Along with his reservations about a monogamous future, there remained one other piece of unfinished business, one very sticky little detail Vince Long still had to take care of before marrying Haley Prentiss. That sticky little detail's name was Candace Ray. They'd met at a Starbucks during Vince's senior year in college, sharing a table one crowded, rainy morning. Candace had a face that drew stares from every male in the room who had a pulse, with legs that didn't quit and a chest to match. Their chance meeting blossomed into a regular daily rendezvous, artfully concealed from Haley who admired Vince's dutiful attention to his studies and his long hours of research at the library. After college, the liaisons continued under the guise of client meetings and catching up with paperwork at the office.

Candace was Vince's female counterpart in every way. The good looks, the subtle cunning, the suave manipulation. They immediately recognized it in each other. Unspoken, it was a case of "I'll use you; you can use me. Let's see how far it takes us until we both get what we want." That is, up to the day at that same Starbucks when Vince made the decision to break things off for good.

"You know you really don't love her. It's all about the money, isn't it? You don't fool me for a second."

"I love her."

46

"You also love me. Remember?"

"I've gotta' do what I've gotta' do."

"You've gotta' do . . . what? That's it? Just like that? Okay. Fine. You'll pay for this, you sonofabitch."

There was something flattering, gratifying about having a woman jealous and angry and being able to walk away from her in front of an audience no less, knowing she still wanted you even as she poured out a torrent of profanity in your direction. But from now on, Vince Long would only look forward. Or so he thought.

*

As they whirled with a flourish around the ballroom floor the night of the wedding, something caught Vince's eyes that made him pause, almost causing Haley to trip.

"What's wrong?"

"Nothing. Nothing at all."

But there was something. Something so unexpected. There stood Candace Ray at the front of the crowd of on looking guests ringing the dance floor. By her side was a man Vince didn't recognize. He had his arm around her waist.

None of this escaped Haley's attention. "Vince, what—or who—are you staring at over there?"

"No. No one. Nothing. Just lost my balance, that's all."

The wedding dance ended, and Vince lost no time pushing Haley back to the head table. As he pulled out her chair and seated her, he looked over her head and across the room. Candace and the unknown partner were now seated at a table alongside the dance floor. What the hell is she up to? How did she manage to get in here, anyway? He already knew the answer—to the second question, at least. She'd used those hard earned people skills of hers the way she always had. But what was her point? Especially since she was there with a date. Was she there to make a scene? Or just to louse up the evening?

"Vince, you seem a thousand miles away. Why don't you at least dance some more with me?"

"Of course."

A minute or two into the next dance, Vince realized the worst of his fears. Candace and her escort were dancing alongside them. Vince attempted to move quickly to the middle of the floor without success. Then over to the other side. Candace and friend followed. It was becoming a wild chase across a crowded dance floor. Haley asked, "Why are you dragging me around like this?"

"I'm not. I just want to get to a clear space where we won't have so many people bumping into us."

The music was winding down now. They were standing in place, still swaying slightly to the rhythm. Vince felt a tap on his schoulder. "May I dance with the bride?"

There was no way to answer the request other than concede. That left Candace standing there, arms open. "Yes, and I get to dance with the lucky groom."

Vince quickly steered his new dance partner away from Haley and the stranger. "What in hell are you up to, Candace?"

"Why, nothing at all. Are you having a good time?

"I was."

"Well, I hope the sight of the woman you really love doesn't ruin your evening. Or your honeymoon."

"Come on. What's this about? And who's the guy?"

"Jealous?"

"Hardly. But does he know about us?"

"He's not the jealous type. And you'd get along good. In fact he's a lot like you. Like both you and me."

"Meaning?"

"We'll leave that to your ever fertile imagination."

She drew herself closely to him. In an instant, the press of her body and the fragrance of

her hair brought back memories and produced stirrings Vince hadn't experienced since they parted. "I just thought maybe the new bride should get to know you better, learn about your past. Especially your recent past."

"And you want to embarrass me here in front of her family and guests? I'd call that a pretty cheesy way to get revenge."

"Oh, don't worry. Nothing's going to happen here. Or tonight. I just wanted to make a sales pitch for some insurance. Did you know I sell insurance now? Life, casualty and liability. I specialize in liability."

Vince stopped short. "You're kidding, right?"

"Not at all."

"Well, if you mean what I think you mean, you can go screw yourself."

"Don't be so crude. Especially now that you're in high society."

The dance ended. Candace held Vince's gaze for several seconds before grasping the hand of her date and disappearing into the crowd.

Back at the table, Haley asked, "How do you know that couple?"

Vince hesitated, not sure what had been said between Haley and the man.

"I don't know him."

"What about her?"

"Not her either. That I can recall, anyway. What did he say to you?"

"He didn't say much. Just that they were your guests and were having a good time."

"Haley my dear, I think our party has just been crashed."

*

In the weeks after returning from the honeymoon, Candace made no reappearance and
Vince was beginning to breathe easier, putting that chapter behind him for good. But on the first Monday of October, not a special day in any other particular way, the chapter reopened the moment Vince picked up the mail at their condominium mailbox.

As Vince headed across the large common area to their townhouse, he tore open the envelope. He didn't often receive personal mail, and this piece, addressed in handwriting he recognized immediately, made him more than a little uneasy. The contents justified his fears.

"Here's hoping all is well with the newlyweds as you settle into your new life. I'm so anxious for us to get together one of these days. The four of us. Dinner? A double date? We have so much in common, and I have so much to share with Haley. Call me when you get a chance. My cell number is the same as always.—Candy."

Vince pocketed the letter in his suit jacket and waited the rest of that evening and the sleepless night that followed before making the call from work.

"Okay, Candace, what do you want?"

"The right question isn't 'what?,' it's 'how much?'"

"I should have known. So get to it."

"I want fifty-thousand."

"You are nuts. Frickin' nuts. I don't have anything like that to give you."

"Please, please. Calm down. We'll gladly take it in installments."

"No, no way. I won't let you bleed me to death. I'd rather she knew about us than give you one fucking dime."

"Okay, then let me spell it out for you." Her voice turned from falsely warm to glacial in an instant. "We know where your parents are, and we'll kill them if you don't come through."

"My parents have been dead for years. I told you that ages ago.

"Come, come. We've found them and they have another 48 hours to live. I need to see the first installment. Five thousand will do."

"You need to see a shrink. That's what you need. A shrink!" He threw his cellphone across his office. A colleague passing his door saw Vince throw it. Newlyweds' first fight he

mused and continued down the hallway towards the water cooler.

*

The following evening, Vince was relieved there were no messages in the mail from Candace. Nothing on his phone, either. Maybe she'd thought better of the idea. His relief was

51

short lived.

"That woman from the wedding was outside on our patio today."

"What woman?"

"The one who danced with you."

"Are you sure . . .? Maybe she lives here. There's hundreds of people living in this complex."

"I'm absolutely certain. She came right up to the door. And she left this for you on the patio table."

It was an unopened manila envelope. Vince grabbed it and started towards the next room. Haley held him back by his shirt sleeve. "Go ahead, open it. Right here, in front of me. I want to know what's going on between the two of you. Now."

Inside were two photographs. One looked to be a man in his mid- to late sixties. The other, a woman of about the same age.

"Who are these people, Vincent?"

"I have absolutely no clue." For once he was being straight with Haley. He'd never laid eyes on either the man or the woman in the photos.

"Haley, you have to believe me. I don't know these people. I don't know this person that's bothering us, either. She's some kind of crazy stalker or something . . .."

"Don't you think we should call the police?"

"And tell them what? That this woman and her partner, boyfriend, husband, whatever, crashed our wedding party and then left photographs of two total strangers on our patio?"

"I think the least we can do is get a security system. Who knows what these people are capable of?"

"Whatever will make you feel safe. Anyway, I'll tell the condo patrol about it. If she shows up again, they'll escort her off the property and that should put an end to it."

*

The next day and evening passed quietly—until the 10 o'clock news. The headline story, complete with yellow police tape, flashing red and blue lights, gurneys and ambulances, was the slaying of an elderly couple in a quiet residential area across town. A neighbor gave the usual impromptu eulogy. "Such a nice couple. Recently retired. A mail man. Always waved. Always smiling. And she was such a dear lady. They didn't have an enemy in the world."

"That's them. The people in the photo." Haley was standing now, shrieking. "And they're dead. Dead." She sat back down and began to shake. "Vince, what do you know about this you aren't telling me?"

"Haley. You know as much as I do. And I know nothing." It was a half-truth—better than an outright lie—and both would have to live with it for now.

*

The first call of the morning had nothing to do with business. At least not the kind of business normally conducted at the offices of Connolly and Barker Wealth Management.

"Candace, what the hell's going on? What have you done to those poor people? I told you I had no parents the first time we met. I was orphaned when I was six."

"Well, you shouldn't take it so hard then. After all, they aren't your flesh and blood. They're just strangers. Perfect strangers."

53

It took Vince several seconds to clear his head and construct a coherent reply. "To me that's just as bad as if they were my parents."

"You mean you've suddenly grown a conscience?"

"You and whoever you're in with are absolutely psycho. And just for grins, who is that

guy you're with, anyway? What's his role in all this?"

"Now, now. I'm not about to incriminate anybody. That wouldn't be nice. But if you must know, he's my baby brother."

"Then it's gotta' be in the family DNA. You must all be crazy."

"We're crazy—about money. But we haven't seen any yet."

"You're not going to, either."

"Now don't get all huffy. Just watch your mail—I wanted to drop something off in person early this morning, but some mean man with a tin badge threatened to call the police. Said I was trespassing. You can't go on hurting my feelings like that, Vinny."

"Don't call me Vinny, don't come near me, stop sending things." He swung around in his chair. Looking through the side light of his closed office door, he saw a line forming of people waiting to see him.

"This conversation is over. Now, get out of my life. For good."

"Watch your mail, sweetheart. Watch your mail."

*

Haley had already been to the mailbox and opened the envelope before Vince arrived home.

The photograph was of a woman in her early twenties. She was pretty, with an engaging smile and that look of innocence you ascribe to someone young who dies tragically, or, in this case, was about to die. On the back, it read, "To my loving brother Vincent, love Sis." The accompanying note demanded ten-thousand dollars by morning, "Five thousand past due. Your sister is okay, for now."

"We both know you have no sister. So, is this girl another anonymous friend of yours from out of the past?"

"Never seen her. I swear."

"Then why do we suddenly have her picture? And a demand for money?"

"Why is any of this happening, Haley?"

"Look, we need to get dad's lawyer involved. He'll figure out how to put a stop to it.

He'll hire a private detective or something. I don't want my family to be connected to any scandal or murders. And you . . . you don't need this either. You're trying to build a client list. This couldn't have come at a worse time."

"Can't we leave well enough alone?"

"Well enough? We have to do something . . ..
"

"Then don't bring your father and his lawyer into this. It'll just make matters worse."

*

Haley would have it no other way. They met that evening with the lawyer and her father, a meeting that turned into a lengthy I-told-you-so session that focused mostly on Vince, tempered only somewhat by his presence in the room. But in the end, they all agreed to do nothing. They salved their collective conscience by writing it off as a bizarre coincidence, a fluke, an amateur

55

attempt to get easy money that would soon go away.

*

The next morning as Vince stood shaving, a news alert began streaming across his iPhone on the bathroom vanity. Looking down at the screen nearly caused him to nick his chin: 23-year-old woman found strangled in mid-city apartment . . . Police looking for clues . . .

The face was fresh in his memory. Too fresh. It was her, the girl in the photo. Vince entered the kitchen, setting the cell phone in front of Haley. She looked up at him, shaking as much as he. "I already saw it on TV. That same girl. Why, Vince? Why?"

*

Vince didn't need to call Candace. She was already holding for him on line three when he entered his office.

"You shouldn't keep me waiting like that. You know how your Sugar Candy hates to wait. For anything—"

"—Whatever it is, get to the point."

"Since you don't seem to want to pay up, others are paying for you . . ."

"Candace, stop the madness. Now!"

"Oh, I plan to. I'm saving the best for last."

"Meaning . . .?

"You'll see, sweetheart. Just watch your mail."

*

Vince made sure to leave the office early, before Haley could have a chance to get the mail. He turned the key in the lock and the mailbox door swung open. Damn. As promised, another envelope from Candace. At least Haley had not seen it first. That was the good news.

56

Now for the bad, he thought, as he moved to one side of the entry and ripped the envelope open. Out slid a photograph of Haley. Haley! It was a glossy, professional photo he'd seen many times. A vanity photo in one of those slightly over the shoulder poses, her head turned towards the camera, hair perfect, light reflecting from smiling eyes. Vince reached for his cell. After a moment, he said, "We need to talk. Now. Starbucks. Be there." Without waiting for a response, he shoved the phone into his pocket and started back towards the condo parking lot.

*

They sat at the only open table in the place, the same table where they sat on that rainy day some three years before. They both realized the irony. Neither said a word about it. Nothing needed be said.

"Just you? Alone? Where's that little brother of yours?"

"I don't need a body guard, do I? Or are you going to kidnap me and tie me up? You liked to tie me up. All the time. Remember?" She moved her chair closer to his so that now their knees were touching. Vince quickly moved his legs away into safer territory and shoved the envelope with Haley's photo across the table.

"Candy, what is it going to take to put an end to this? You can't be serious. . ."

"The ball, as they say, is in your court."

"I can't come up with the kind of money you want. Not now. Someday, yes."

"That's okay, lover. I had another idea. Maybe . . . maybe you and I can form some kind of . . . some kind of partnership . . ."

Her last words hung in the air, and now their knees were touching again. Vince got up to

57

leave. Unlike the last time he had departed from Candace at that Starbucks, there was silence between them.

*

Vince Long left the parking lot and drove towards the freeway. He thought about what had just happened. What he felt when he saw Candace sitting at that table. About what had been said. And what had passed between them without being said. He thought about Haley, the money, the houses, the cars, the travel, the status. Then, his thoughts raced back to Candace. He drove a few more blocks and pulled over to the curb. He removed Haley's photograph from the envelope. He stared at it several seconds before he began tearing it into pieces. He tore the bigger pieces into smaller pieces. Slowly, deliberately. He gathered the pieces into one hand. With the other he steered the car back onto the street and pushed open the sunroof. As he reached the freeway ramp, he raised the hand with the pieces through the opening. He sped up the ramp, releasing his grip and watching in the rear view mirror as the fragments of Haley Prentiss' image scattered like frightened doves, disappearing forever against an incredibly blue afternoon sky.

***

©2019 John Timm

58

الضوضاء والتسرع

Amid the Noise & Haste

J.D. Graves

Bud's work phone had twenty-three missed calls and counting. He'd left it in the truck outside the Sunny Acres retirement community. At fifty-five dollars an hour, Bud cranked the plumber's snake into the brown water slowly. Of course, it wasn't just his hourly rate that slowed his progress. This particular job demanded a certain caution that Bud Sanders had never quite mastered.

"You're doing it again!" Mrs. Grieves cried from the doorway of the tiny bathroom.

"Ma'am?" Bud paused his cranking.

The old lady shook her walker in fury, "You're getting too close to My Precious!"

Bud quickly scanned the toilet-tank's top, and the sink's rim, and the ridge of the tub, and even the towel rack. Bud hesitated, "Which one of your sweet things am I bothering, exactly?"

"My Precious!" Mrs. Grieves fumed, "She doesn't like people and I can't guarantee she won't scratch your eyes out. Don't get any closer." Bud nodded trying to pinpoint exactly which of the hundreds of small porcelain cats worried Mrs. Grieves.

"Yes ma'am," Bud said. "Are you sure you won't reconsider letting me herd them from harm's way? At least, no one would get their eyes scratched."

"They're taking their naps," Mrs. Grieves said, "If Shadow, and Tiger-Lily, and Chance, and Kitty Kate don't get their naps they'll be up all-night meowing at the door. I won't get a wink of sleep."

Bud choked back a laugh. Deep below the brown abyss, he felt the tip of the auger halt against some pipe monster. Bud couldn't be sure if he'd found the trouble or not. He wiggled the snake gently, "Keep you up a lot do they?"

"Oh, yes! Especially if they don't get their medicine," Mrs. Grieves said. "Mr. Cleveland and Mrs. Figteeth can wake the dead coughing up hairballs."

The blockage eased slightly. An air bubble surfaced and popped, releasing aromatic flavors of old urine, feces, and infection. The stench gagged Bud. He let go of the handle and the damn thing stood on its own. He'd never seen anything like it. Almost hypnotic the way the handle stood erect, gently keeping time side to side. Bud gripped his hips and giggled to himself. "Well, ain't that something special." Whatever was stuck in the pipe, Bud knew was just the beginning of his troubles.

"Don't dawdle! Finish your business!" Mrs. Grieves commanded, "It's not proper having strangers invading my privacy. Disturbing my cats. I'm calling the manager!"

"Ma'am," Bud said, "for the last time, the managers who *called me.* You complained your toilet wouldn't flush. Maybe you should use less paper. Do this old world a favor and save a few trees."

Mrs. Grieves cried, "This is an *outrage!"*

"I've seen it a thousand times," Bud smiled. "A few squares will do just as good as a whole roll. Front to back twice and your undercarriage's as clean as most folks."

"You're trying to distract me!" Mrs. Grieves growled, "You're working with the nurses aren't you? They're always finding ways to distract. They're always stealing my things! That's how I lost my glasses. That's how I lost my teeth! I'm registering a complaint!"

Bud shook the auger. A few brown droplets splashed from the bowl. He half expected to hear Mrs. Grieves shout another complaint, but when he checked, her old bones had disappeared. Bud glimpsed her bent shape slowly shuffling from the room. The portable oxygen tank squeaked behind her into the hallway.

"Time to get the wrinkles out of your sunshine," Bud told himself. "Come on baby take the bait, ain't no one here but me and you," Bud gently flopped the job up and down until he felt a bite. He gripped the handle with both hands, "Patience old Bud. No need to rock the boat. Reel it in nice and slow. Don't crack this pipe. You ain't too keen on sailing back out to help crazy cat ladies unclog their commodes."

The auger wouldn't budge.

Fresh sweat slowly dripped from Bud's temple.

Bud's clock ticked. He gritted his teeth and pulled again. Nothing moved. He pictured a strange combination of muddy reading glasses and soiled dentures smiling at him from inside the pipe. They mocked him and Bud—just couldn't tolerate mockery—real or imagined.

"To hell with this," Bud said and forced the snake up and down rapidly. Water sloshed everywhere. A gleeful mess as Bud laughed aloud, "I know I hooked ya!"

The commode gurgled and Bud yanked back hard. The darkness sank. Crystal clear water refilled the bowl.

Bud should've seen it coming. He held the dripping hook eye level. "What did that old widow name your sorry self?"

The figurine must've been in the pipe awhile as some of the Tabby's paint had peeled. The yellow of its eyes had all but dissolved. He thought about throwing it in the trash, but then he thought about the old woman's face as she opened a gift from a grandchild. He wondered if that grandchild even visited anymore. How quickly children grow up and leave you with your memories and their junk. Bud rinsed the cat off and replaced it among its peers. After all, in the plumbing game, Sunny Acres and other establishments like her, were easy marks. It's hard to make a living no matter what you do. No need to go out of the way to kill the golden goose.

Bud grabbed the bathmat and blotted away most of the spillage. He kicked the mat back into place and washed his hands. He collected his things and headed out the door.

The front desk overlooked the activity area. Several former and future clients milled about playing checkers and watching television. Bud good naturedly approached the fat day clerk. She had Pam scrawled on her nametag and distractedly said, "It's hard to get 'em out once they reach that point."

"Just another day—another dollar," Bud smiled. "Now I'll never talk someone outta giving me money for my labor—but this job could be categorized as preventative maintenance. You'll need to say something about the resident's collectibles being in places they shouldn't."

Pam looked at him blank, "Huh?"

"The clog in room Seven A. One of them figurines had fallen in," Bud said. "I'm still gonna have to charge you for the full hour. Company policy. I hope you understand. Now I'd be willing to wave the equipment fee, if you guys pay cash."

"Oh, I wasn't talking about that," Pam said.

"Then what's clouding over your day darling?"

"You haven't seen the news yet?"

Bud glanced over his shoulder, "Who's got time for all that nonsense?"

"Time's all we got around this place," Pam said.

Bud nodded and produced his receipt book. He scribbled in it, "What happened? Another building blow up?"

"Not this time," Pam said. "It seems we got two Good Samaritans over in a warzone got themselves kidnapped. They was over there helping with the Red Cross or something."

"You don't say," Bud stopped writing. He shook his head in disgust. "I blame their dad-gum parents for not spanking them when they were little. That'd fix alot of the world's issues right there. Keep a lotta good people out of bad places."

"I don't know. They look like babies themselves," Pam said. "It's a terrible shame such good looking twin brothers are being messed up like this."

Bud squinted at the screen across the room, "Twin's you say?"

"Yeah," Pam said, "News says they's from here in Middlebury. I think they's went to school with my brother."

Bud felt suddenly heavy and empty at the same time. Surely it was only a coincidence. Surely there existed more than one set of twins in Middlebury who just happened to go to--"Which country did you say they were in?"

"Africa some place," Pam said. Her voice already fading behind him as a current pushed him forward. The absurdity of the cascading words: kidnapped and ransomed, floated away from Bud. He mindlessly moved into the activity room. The talking heads mouthed the words, "Our government does not negotiate with terrorists."

Bud hovered inches from the video loops of his son's faces. All the air escaped him. Tears wetted his cheeks. He gripped his knees. Some old geezer behind him yelled, "Sit down you moron I can't see!" And another added, "You make a better door than a window!" And yet another said, "Change the channel, it's almost time for Jeopardy."

*

Dusty sat facing away from the television. She didn't want to look. She didn't want to be sucked back into that particular vortex. Eyes glued to the screen as the grainy video looped. Their faces scruffy and dirtied. The assault rifles raised. The assailants masked. Over everyone's heads, a black banner in a strange language Dusty could not read. Below them, white letters on red scrolled quickly, *Breaking News: Two Americans Held Hostage by Jihadi Militant Splinter Cell.*

The phone had rung out all morning. Now the receiver waited on the counter next to its stand. A tinny voice squawking incoherently and uninterrupted. Dusty ignored her sister's rushed babble. She took her time opening the orange pill bottle. She chased two Diazepam and one Ultram with a glass of pinot noir. She placed the empty glass next to the phone and braced for impact. Dusty held the receiver to her ear and spoke flat, "Max certainly looked tired. Michael not so much, but I don't think either is getting much sleep. Do you Rose?"

Rose broke in, "They've probably been kept awake for days!"

65

Dusty went on absently, "Well, maybe they're able to nap every now and then."

"Dusty! I don't understand why you're so calm about this—your son's are being tortured!"

Dusty sighed, "I do hope they're getting enough water. It gets awfully hot over there. I'd hate for them to overheat. You know what they say about dehydrating, you can never push yourself to such extremes again. And you know how Max loves playing tennis..."

A loud crackle filled Dusty's ear as Rose screeched a response. Whatever Dusty's sister said didn't register, nor did it matter. Dusty knew that as soon as she ended the call, another would ring, and then another, and then another after that. She'd thought about disconnecting it from the wall, but then she'd be forced to deal with this entire ordeal herself. She knew she couldn't shoulder this load alone. Especially since her husband, Bud, still hadn't returned. *How long had it been?*

Once home, Dusty thought, Bud would be in a state for sure.

Dusty glanced over at the sunlight streaking through the shuttered windows. She pictured Bud, cursing and spitting, as he was forced to park at least two streets over. Then of course there'd be more cursing and spitting, as her husband of twenty-five years three months and fourteen days, navigated the reporter's blockade outside their home. She meant, her home.

A future event as clear as the empty wine glass next to her phone's cradle. If only she could've been this prescient six months ago. Before she'd watched her boys pack their bags. Before she alone drove them to the airport. Before she'd kissed each one goodbye. *If I'd*

*known this would happen I'd have made sure
they packed extra underwear and socks.*

Now, cocooned in the safety of her suburban
floorplan, Dusty indulged the frantic callers--
family, friends, and neighbors. All of their heartfelt
condolences. All of their righteous outrage. All of
their crackling histrionics. A constant white noise
chorus, "What are you and Bud gonna do about
the twins?"

"Oh my God Dusty! CNN's outside your
house!" Dusty heard Rose say, "You shouldn't be
alone—I'm coming over!"

"That's not necessary. Bud'll surely be here
any minute, and besides..." Rose's dialtone
clicked over. Gently, Dusty placed the receiver
beside its base, taking much care to avoid re-
cradling it.

She smiled to herself—it seems, someone
had mercifully refilled her wine glass. She didn't
bother to look around. Dusty had her suspects
and she was grateful. Of course, the glass didn't
stay full for long.

The uncradled phone's dialtone roared angry
echoes, like atonal katydids on summer nights. *A
loud, off-key, repetition for attention.* For a
moment, Dusty Sanders *rejoiced* in the staccato
noise. *At least,* she told herself, *it no longer rang.*

*

Outside Sanders Plumbing Supply, the media
swarmed. Despite this, Bud charged ahead like a
heavy breeze. A dark-haired reporter bounced
backwards to keep ahead of him, "This is
important news! Two All American boys
sacrificing their lives to save others. People want
to know their real story. America has a right to
know their favorite brand of breakfast cereal,"
The reporter suddenly collided with a

67

backpedaling cameraman. They collapsed and vanished under the trampling mob. A replacement appeared immediately, shoving a microphone at Bud's nose.

"Did your son's cross the Tanzanian border? Is that why they were kidnapped?"

"I have no clue," Bud growled and slapped away the microphone.

A female reporter velcroed herself to Bud's side, "Hi, Maggie Dean, Channel 7. Did you know you were sending your children into a war zone?"

"I don't know—my wife made all the arrangements."

"Ever heard of the Islamic Courts Union before today?"

"No," Bud pushed on.

Another voice in the cacophony of voices, "Is it true your son's were secretly working for Al-Ribat in a pay for food scheme that went bad?"

"Who's Al Ribbad?" Bud asked, "Never heard of him."

"Mr. Sanders do you plan on paying the ransom?"

"Have the terrorists contacted you personally?"

"Mr. Sanders can you answer our questions?"

"Mr. Sanders!" *Mr. SANDERS! Mister...!*

Bud feared he be crushed right there in front of God and Main Street Traffic. Suddenly, a hand grip him from behind. He went sprawling. Pain shot through his face as his cheek skidded across the concrete floor. He looked back just in time to see Jerri-Lynn slam the front door behind them. Her multi-colored nail polish twisted a wad of keys at the lock and hit the light switch. She flipped the *Sorry We're Closed* sign into place. The clock above her read: 10:35 AM.

Faces, cameras and questions pressed against the glass from outside. Jerri-Lynn turned to Bud and puffed deep on a cigarette. Even in the dim, her make-up looked painted on with a trowel. Her blue eyeshadow sparkled like dust from a stripper's thigh. Her white top barely covered the stack of dark bra beneath. She adjusted the yellow bandana around her neck and ashed the cigarette on the floor. "I know NOW may not be the best time to talk about this," Jerri-Lynn cocked her hip, "But after that rescue—you need to seriously consider giving me a raise."

Bud got to his knees wordlessly.

Jerri-Lynn pulled the window's shade, plunging the pair further into business dark. Bud slumped into a chair along the wall of pictures frames. He hung his head in his hands. Jerri-Lynn peaked out the shade and said, "They've been calling all morning. One tried to sneak in and set up his camera. Told me he was with the water department. I kicked his credentials to the curb. Tried to warn you too, but someone never picks up the phone."

Bud patted his pants, "Must still be in the truck."

A camera flashed at her and she shut the blinds, "If they want ransom money. You may be able to call one of them charities or something. Maybe there's even a government program." Bud Shook his head, "I don't even know where to begin."

"I know it's none of my business," Jerri-Lynn said and lit a cigarette. "But the first thing you need to do's go see Dusty."

Bud glared at her, then turned around and removed one of the framed pictures off the wall revealing the safe. He punched in Dusty's birthday and it opened.

Jerri-Lynn blew out a cloud, "What are you looking for?"

"Paperwork. I might need to borrow some cash against my life insurance." Bud pulled out a nickel-plated revolver and set it on the desk.

"That's some life insurance policy you got Bud. You're not planning on showing that to the crowd outside are you? They'll have you arrested for violating the second amendment."

Bud didn't respond and kept digging in the safe.

"I'd suggest you leave it here when you go see your wife."

Bud grunted and sat at his desk, "That's dumber than hell. I ain't doing no such thing."

"You know you ain't getting out of it. Despite everything that's happened, those boys are her children same as yours. Just go and get it over with. I still be here for you when you done."

"I ain't got nothing to say to Dusty without a lawyer present..."

The backdoor squealed open. Both Bud and Jerri-Lynn turned to look at the vision in pink who had invaded the office. Her blue eyes twinkled just like the diamonds on her ears, neck, and wrists. Her full pink lips parted, "Hello, the back door was opened. I hope you don't mind that I let myself in. I'm Betty-Lou Buckingham. Maybe you voted for my husband, Congressman Joe Don 'Buck' Buckingham?"

Bud squinted with confusion.

"Oh, Mr. Sanders, you poor dear!" At once, this stranger wrapped her bracelets around his neck. She smelled real special. Her voice swooned, "I cannot imagine what you and your family are going through right now. I've prayed about it all day long. Do you hear me? All day."

Betty-Lou gripped his shoulders firmly, "I told Buck this morning, after we learned that your boys were from our district. I said Buck, we just have to do something to help our people. So, I flew out immediately."

"You flew?" Jerri-Lynn stammered, "to Middlebury?"

"You must be Mrs. Sanders. Where are my manors?" She hugged Jerri-Lynn stiffly, "It's very nice to meet you Rusty."

"Dusty...and I ain't her."

Bud cleared his throat, "She's my...my secretary--my wife's probably at her house...your husband's a Congressman?"
Betty-Lou clucked her tongue knowingly. Her eyes bounced between the two of them. Her polished hand lightly touched Bud's. Her fingers, oddly cold, "Has anyone from the state department, or any official, other than myself contacted any of you?"

Bud and Jerri-Lynn shook their heads.
She stood. Her words propelled her pace back and forth, "Typical, just typical. I swear the federal government couldn't fill a bucket of water if it was thirsty. Leave it to those Washington fat cats to make good Christian people like myself deliver bad news. Of course, it goes without saying the terrorist'll ask for a $100 million. Don't worry that's just a negotiation tactic. Always ask for the moon first, you'll never get a second chance. Basic strategy."

"A hundred million what...dollars?" Bud asked.

"Don't worry," Betty-Lou said. "All negotiations will be handled through third party affiliates. Uncle Sam doesn't deal with these matters directly. Leaves it all to non-profits and private entities. For example, the Yellow-Ribbon Brigade has handled such issues before...Do you remember those two girls kidnapped by Somali pirates last year?"

Bud drew a blank.

"Doesn't matter," Betty-Lou smiled, "the point is we got them home and it only cost the family around forty million."

Bud nearly fell out of his chair, "I don't have forty million—I barely got twenty bucks on me now."

"That's where I come in—well more exactly, my organization. The Yellow-Ribbon Brigade raises money for American citizens who find themselves outside of diplomatic assistance. I've been a member since I graduated law school. I'm also a past President. Let's just say, your family and the family of the third hostage, is very lucky that I found you. But I'm gonna be frank, we're facing a definite time crunch here..."
"There's a third?" Bud asked.

Betty-Lou didn't answer. The wall mounted with pictures had caught her attention. Bud watched her move from frame to frame. Finally, she spoke softly, "This is perfect...absolutely perfect. Why you can't make this up...you're a Little League sponsor?"

Bud nodded, "Every year for over a decade."

"Are your son's in any of these photos?"

"Yeah a couple...why do you...?"

Betty-Lou grabbed one off its nail and turned around, "You'll need as many pictures as you can find. Even if you sign up with one of the lessor organizations—they'll need them for the TV bumps. You'd never believe how many of those scab groups forget that particular attention to detail. As if they're only in it for their cut of ten percent and not in it for the rescue of American children. Be careful Mr. Sanders..." Her eyes and earlobes pleaded, "You're gonna wanna go with someone you can trust to handle this situation professionally."

Jerri-Lynn put out her cigarette, "Ten percent? That don't sound very charitable. How much are we talking here?"

The woman kept her focus on Bud, "In order to maximize the donations--you'll need to make sure your boys appear as real live human beings. Their story is your story. It's the key to getting them back home. The most important thing in the world. Don't forget that—especially when the silly ungodly numbers start flying around. I mean, a million here—a million there. It's very easy to get lost if you don't have a guide to show you the way."

Betty-Lou handed Bud the picture. It was the only one without any of his sons on the team— but he understood the gesture completely.

Bud smiled. He knew exactly what needed to be done. He'd been worried about seeing Dusty again—stressing about whether to bring her flowers or what type of flowers or if he should go empty handed—but now it did not matter. *Fuck flowers* Bud had Betty-Lou.

"This is all seems so sudden...Mrs. Buckingham."

"Please Bud call me Betty-Lou."

He played it cool, "I'm gonna need to discuss all of this with Dusty."

"Bud, I know I'm a complete stranger...but in desperate times I believe in miracles, don't you?" Betty-Lou went to the door. Her taxi waited for them outside in the alley. "Why don't the two of you ride over with me and we can discuss how best to approach the situation."

Bud set the team photo on the desk next to the gun and raised an eyebrow at Jerry-Lynn. His secretary shrugged and stood and followed the stranger to the outside.

*

Mike Sanders had an itch he just couldn't scratch. It stung him in the dead center of his back. He prayed a bead of sweat would roll just the right way and extinguish it. He shifted his manacled hands back and forth but only drew the notice of the guard. A kid no older than Mike stared at his prisoner with knives for eyes. The kid held the AK-47 in one hand, with the other he drew something out of the teal fanny pack. Mike stilled and looked away. No comfort could be found sitting like this in the dirt. Although his makeshift cuffs gave a little, they Scrooged back most of the slack. Mike figured some guys have all the luck—guys like his brother Max and to a lesser extent—their youth minister, Stephen.

Last night, Brother Stephen whispered to Mike he'd discovered buried treasure. Just below his hands lived a gift from God. "I don't know exactly what blessing has befallen me, but Brother it's hard and sharp enough, I might be able to break through the plastic on my wrists."

After a few more moments of investigation he whispered, "I think it's a broken shovel...It would make as much sense as anything else in this shithole."

Their makeshift prison wasn't more than a forgotten tool shed. Corrugated tin rusted all around the six prisoners, three Americans—three others of local origin, scattered across the dirt

74

floor. A few farming implements clung to nails above their heads.

From the corner of his eye, Mike watched the kid guard clutch a square of paper. The boy never took his eyes off Mike as he rolled himself a cigarette. The army fatigues slouched off the boy's thin frame. The Leopard spot sash made him look like the kid Mayor of Elephant Dung Africa, population unknown. The boy took a small knife off the table and packed the ends of the cigarette with it. He returned the knife, pinched the cigarette between his lips and struck a match. He stood there idly smoking. The blue fog wreathed his whisker free face. The kid mayor resembled a young lion ordering off a lunch menu.

The door to the shed squealed open. In walked an older guard—naked to the waist save for the leopard spotted sash. The kid mayor offered him his cigarette, but the shirtless guard declined and said, "Nipa moja."

The kid mayor grunted unhappily, before returning to his fanny pack and rolling two more. Once he'd completed this task, he placed the knife in his belt. The older man clapped the kid mayor on the shoulder and led the boy outside.

Mike watched them exit with candid relief. It was the first time they'd been alone since Lake Victoria. Where the three of them, Brother Stephen and Max, had gone for a swim and ended up hogtied. Max had tried to overpower the Leopard people but a quick slap with an AK-47 had knocked him cold. Now Mike's twin brother lay unconscious and crumpled in the corner.

"Psst!" Brother Stephen whispered, "Mike! I've almost got my hands free."

Mike nodded with wide eyed anticipation.

"Once I'm free I'm gonna take one of those pick axes over by the table and we're getting out of here." Stephen looked at the other prisoners and added, "All of us."

Brother Stephen frantically sawed his arms. Outside, Mike could hear the Leopard People talking and smoking. Mike still couldn't scratch his itch. Max remained unmoved. There was a muted pop and Brother Stephen leapt to his feet. Looked at his freed hands then back at the opened door.

Maybe it was fear—maybe the adrenaline, but Mike couldn't understand Stephen's next choice. Mike whispered, *"Brother Stephen?"*

Stephen didn't respond. Quietly, the youth minister crept to a row of rusty farm implements over the table. He reached but couldn't gain purchase. At once, Mike saw Stephen's target. Some antique hatchet, its wooden handle long lost and forgotten. Stephen heaved himself onto the table. Slowly, he stood as the thing shook beneath him.

"Stephen don't!"

The table squealed as the leg buckled and sent the youth minister crashing to ground.

Outside, the guards stopped talking.

Stephen screamed and grabbed his knee. Blood darkened the orange jumpsuit. Two shadows filled the doorway.

The shirtless guard picked Stephen up in one smooth motion and dropped him in front of Mike. The Kid Mayor pulled Stephen's head back. The guards screamed at each other and pointed. Everything happened so fast. Stephen choked and gurgled as the knife ran left to right across his throat.

76

***

©2019 J.D. Graves

The Radical Mr. Bogota

by Alec Cizak

Mr. Bogata told Armen Faulk to put on his seatbelt. He said, "This is where we drop the hammer." He'd passed the black SUV with *Life Moments Photography* written in red, cursive letters on the driver's side door. The woman behind the wheel had glanced over, her forehead wrinkled, no doubt confused. Considering the icy roads, she'd been cruising as fast as anyone could reasonably expect.

At least, that's what Armen imagined the woman had been thinking.

Mr. Bogata spun his Dodge Dart a hundred and eighty degrees and stopped. He put his left foot on the brake and revved the engine with his right. "Just look at her," he said. He flipped his Spandau Ballet-bangs over his ear. "Just *bathing* in privilege while you fucking starve."

Armen hadn't considered it in such terms. He needed to pay Lake County Gas and Electric or they'd shut off the heat in his apartment. His wife had just given birth to their first child, Shona. When he'd explained the situation to Mr. Bogata at work, asked if Mr. Bogata's dad could give him an advance on his salary, Mr. Bogata babbled about proletariats and the bourgeoisie. He'd said, "Ain't that like this shitty, messed up world?" He'd been marching through the aisles at his father's cement factory, making sure nobody goofed off. "Early funds from the old man? No can do," he said. "But I'll tell you what we *can* do." And that's when he made the proposal. Armen hadn't been too keen, but he went along, fueled by the threat of his family freezing to death.

"You sure she'll cave?" he said to Mr. Bogata as he buckled his seatbelt. The Dart was brand new. Should have kept him safe. But maybe, just maybe, the woman in the SUV might be stubborn.

"She ain't got what I got." Mr. Bogata pounded himself in the chest and put the car in drive. He flipped his bangs again. His shampoo filled the air with a flowery, chemical odor. Ice beneath the wheels scattered as he released the brakes. Banks of snow created by a county plow narrowed the road to one lane. Beyond mini-mountain ranges lining the slick pavement, sugar-coated treetops hinted at the depths of the ravines on both sides. "Better hold on to something," said Mr. Bogata.

The woman craned over her steering wheel. She slapped the horn several times. She did *not* slow down.

Mr. Bogata stomped the gas pedal. The needle on the speedometer approached sixty. Armen's pale knuckles clutched the 'oh shit' handle above his door. "Maybe I can take a loan from the bank," he said, hoping Mr. Bogata would abort the mission.

Mr. Bogata parroted dialogue from *Fight Club*, dime store Buddhist bullshit about "living in the moment," and leaned back. His grip on the steering wheel reminded Armen of the old Maxell print ad of a guy holding onto a couch as though it were a roller coaster. Sammy Hagar, or some other gaudy radio rock from the 1980s, would have completed the scene. Mr. Bogata's iPhone, plugged into the car stereo, however, played nothing but mono-rhythmic electronica. "Besides," he said, "what bank's going to draw up a loan for a few hundred bucks?"

As they approached the SUV and the driver of the SUV refused to budge, Armen said, "How about *you* loan me the money, bro?"

"*Bro*?" Mr. Bogata sneered. "I'm your fucking *boss*. Don't forget that."

The woman driving the SUV snapped her steering wheel to the side. The oversized station wagon spun onto two wheels and then flipped over an embankment. Mr. Bogata slowed and turned around. He brought the car to a stop at a cavity the SUV had punched through the wall of snow. "I'll chew off my left nut if that broad's in any condition to stop us now." He got out and started down the side of the ravine.

Armen felt nauseous. Even when Mr. Bogata had suggested the *Life Moments* photographer could solve Armen's problems, Armen hadn't believed they'd go through with it. Mr. Bogata explained his sister Eva had revealed underclass pictures were scheduled for Haggard High that day. Mr. Bogata said the photographer collected cash only. "She'll have four, maybe five hundred dollars," he'd said. "We can split it. You can pay your stupid bill and take your wife to a Bears game or something." Armen argued with him, initially. Mr. Bogata reminded him of their time in high school—"You used to sell weed for me, remember?"

Armen had had *nothing* to do with drugs since senior year. For whatever reason, however, his manager bringing up their former business relationship compelled him to go along with the plan. Didn't seem so serious, anyway. Mr. Bogata described the *Life Moments* photographer as a bourgeois fat cat stealing money from poor parents and students in exchange for a phony memento, a flimsy piece of nostalgia designed, as he stated it, "to dupe folks into thinking their lives have more meaning than they actually do."

After Armen agreed to participate, Mr. Bogata dropped more politics. He called it "a complete lack of fairness" that a woman driving a fancy SUV should go home with an envelope full of money and no problems on her shoulders. "Privileged whore," he'd said, sitting in the Dart, across the street from Haggard High, watching the pear-shaped woman load ten crates of lights and camera equipment into the SUV by herself. When she walked around the driver's side, she cradled a yellow envelope under her arm, held onto it as though it contained a map to the Holy Grail. The holes in her shoes and the frayed ends of her pants legs suggested membership in the struggling class.

*

Armen got out of the Dart and followed Mr. Bogata into the ravine. The SUV rested, upside down, across freezing water. Steam rose around it, no doubt the result of different, colliding temperatures. The woman must not have worn her seat belt. She'd been tossed through the windshield and landed, limbs crooked, a few feet from the creek. Armen said, "We need to call an ambulance."

"Are you stupid?" Mr. Bogata didn't look at him when he spoke.

"We can call anonymous."

"Don't be so naïve." Mr. Bogata squatted by the SUV. He cleared broken class from the ceiling and rummaged through a stack of papers. He found the envelope and stood. As he stuffed it inside his jacket, he said, "Sweet."

The woman rolled over and screamed. Her chest heaved in rapid bursts, stopping and starting, as though her respiratory system were an engine refusing to fire. Armen recognized her then. He'd seen her several times at Goodwill, going through racks of clothes, just like his wife did any time they had an extra nickel or two at the end of the month.

"She's gone," said Mr. Bogata. He headed up the embankment, toward the road.

Armen stared at the company logo on the door of the SUV, crumpled from the accident. He wondered, for just a moment, what kind of car the woman *actually* owned.

Mr. Bogata started the Dart and honked the horn. As Armen climbed over the embankment, Mr. Bogata rolled down the passenger-side window. "Let's motor, bro'!"

Armen got into the car. He struggled with his seatbelt. His hands wouldn't stop shaking. Maybe his instincts were wrong. Maybe Mr. Bogata had been correct. Maybe the woman *had* been wealthy. Maybe she stood on her feet for eight hours, wrangling snotty teenagers, tolerating fussy parents, because she was bored. She'd inherited millions of dollars and decided she wanted to wallow with the doomed. But he knew no such reality existed. To drown nagging voices in his mind, he spoke. "You count the money?"

"What's it matter?"

"I still need to pay the heat bill," said Armen.

"Yeah, yeah." Mr. Bogata shuffled through songs on his iPhone, landed on another dance tune that sounded like all the others. "Let's head back to my place, play some *Madden*."

A headache lingered near the top of Armen's brain, threatened to drape itself across the front of his skull. "I have to get home, bro…" He stopped himself. "*Mr.* Bogata, I mean," he said. "I have to get home, give my wife some time off."

83

"Yeah, yeah," said Mr. Bogata. "Relax. You just made some easy money. Like the old days, you dig?"

Selling weed in high school had *not* been easy. Even then, Mr. Bogata insisted on being called Mr. Bogata, as opposed to his first name, Howard. He once revealed to Armen he thought Howard made him sound like an overweight retired guy in a fishing cap and Hawaiian shirt. He'd float Armen an ounce of pot and expect him to sell it within a day. If Armen couldn't move the entire stash, Mr. Bogata charged him interest. Just when Armen had gotten fed up with the arrangement, just when he'd decided to tell Mr. Bogata he quit, the school turned Third Reich on him. Haggard PD brought in Nazi dogs to sniff lockers. Sure enough, they smelled dope he'd hidden behind his chemistry book. The school's new administration wanted to look tough, so they kicked him out. He had to finish online and go through life with a GED instead of a full-fledged high school diploma. Had Mr. Bogata ever apologized for that? Admitted to some culpability? No. And when Mr. Bogata suggested he could get him a job at the cement factory, he promised there'd be no hoops to jump through. That didn't stop Mr. Bogata's dad from grilling Armen in the interview, insisting he submit to a urine test every six weeks. Had Armen not met and married Larissa Farmer, he might have gone bonkers and morphed into one of those psychopaths who announce their resignations with an assault rifle. Now he had a daughter, and that daughter had, until that very moment, anchored him to sanity.

"All right," he said. He knew Mr. Bogata wouldn't split the money with him if he didn't give

him a chance to clobber him in *Madden* a few
times. He sat back and pretended the steady
thumping from the speakers in the doors of the
Dart didn't exist. He imagined listening to
something less repetitive, like folk music from the
old country, stuff his grandpa used to play on
records at Christmastime.

*

Mr. Bogata's bedroom in his father's house
was bigger than Armen's apartment. The walls
were covered with posters of Mao, Che Guevara,
and several MMA fighters. Mr. Bogata had
connected his Xbox to an LCD projector aimed at
a wall. They sat on a couch beneath it. "Here you
go." Mr. Bogata handed him a controller with a
loose left knob. He fired up *Madden* and chose
the Patriots.

Armen went with the Bears, knowing full well
they were terrible and he'd watch the computer
version of Tom Brady throw one pass after
another to streaking receivers the Bears'
defensive backs couldn't compete with; On
several occasions, he claimed the offensive line
had gotten away with blatant holding. Mr. Bogata
called him a "hater," and suggested Armen select
a better team the next time they played.

"My family have always been Bears fans,"
said Armen. "I'm not going to change my
allegiance just because they're going through
hard times."

Mr. Bogata insisted Armen indulge a best-of-
three series with him and then made him endure
a third contest despite having won the first two by
blowouts. The sun outside Mr. Bogata's picture
windows faded. Armen said, "I got to get home,
give my wife a rest."

"That's cool." Mr. Bogata shut off the Xbox and started for his bedroom door.

"Can we split the money?" said Armen.

"Jesus!" Mr. Bogata nodded like a bobblehead doll. "Money's not the most important thing in life," he said. "You ever think about people in third world shitholes? How tough they got it?" He snapped his fingers at him like a dog. "Let's go." He looked like Armen's father had the day Armen had been kicked out of Haggard High for possession of marijuana.

*

In the car, cruising through downtown Haggard, Armen looked over at Mr. Bogata, trying to formulate a diplomatic way to ask exactly when the money would be divided. Red lights from Dairy Queen and the Princess movie theater glowed on freshly fallen snow.

Mr. Bogata snapped at him. "What?" he said. "What is it?"

"I don't mean to be rude," said Armen. "I just think we should split up the cash. I mean, a woman died, probably, I mean, just so I can pay my heat bill…"

"Money, money, money," said Mr. Bogata. He shook his head with a pained grimace, reminded Armen of yappers on political news channels, feigning outrage at something their ideological opponents had posted on *Twitter*. "All right, you greedy son of a bitch." Mr. Bogata turned the steering wheel hard and pulled onto a gravel road leading to Baco Bridge, a trestle across Lake Arthur adorned with the letters B, A, C, O, and S by the town's stoners in the mid-1980s. He stopped the car, got out, and trudged onto the train tracks.

86

Armen stumbled through the snow after him, wishing he had the guts to grab the envelope and run. He joined Mr. Bogata at the middle of the trestle.

"Your materialism is poisonous," said Mr. Bogata. He took the envelope from his jacket pocket and thumbed through the stack of money inside it. "The best thing I can do for you, I think, is teach you to worry about more important things." And then he turned the envelope over and dumped its contents. Individual bills fluttered to the lake below like dying birds.

Armen thought of diving after them. The freezing water would probably kill him. His feet sank into gravel between the railroad ties. His body chilled as an early evening wind reminded him people were waiting on him, depending on him.

***

©2019 Alec Cizak

THE ALIBI

Robb T. White

Jack Frielander sat midway down the bar in the Coyote Den watching the new girl do her set. She had a sleeve of tattoos; the outlined bump at the crotch of her neon-yellow thong showed she shaved down there. He had a buzz going although it was still afternoon. Without letting the bartender catch him, he riffled through the bills on the bar, figuring he was good for two more shots, hold the chasers, and cut back on the tip. Frielander couldn't remember the last time he had money in his pocket to drink all night and buy rounds.

"Cash Money"!

Jack hadn't heard his nickname in ten years. His crew supervisor last night slipped up and called him "Freeloader." The punk was the son of the owner of the construction company where he'd been forced to take a clean-up job or lose his welfare. He shrugged off the "accidental" slip but burned inside.

Jackie's neck swiveled to take in the newcomer standing inside the door backlit by the low lighting; he couldn't make out any features to tell who it was.

The man approached just as Jackie reassembled the guy's features like unscrambling the pixels of a once-familiar face now transplanted onto an older man, someone his own age. The man gave him a friendly wallop between the shoulder blades just as the penny dropped: Pete Ramos.

"Jackie Frielander, look at you, man," Ramos said and hoisted himself onto the seat beside him. He made enough commotion to knock Jackie's arm and spill some of the precious amber liquid.

"Pete Ramos, son of a gun," Jackie said, thinking, *son of a bitch* instead, but falling short of the hail-fellow-well-met tone he aimed for.

"What have you been up to since high school?"

Fuck a duck, there goes the rest of my short night. Jackie knew he had zero chance of ogling the girls after the newbie, two spectacular babes.

"Oh, you know, this and that, nothing much," Jackie replied.

Again, the levity wasn't there, but he hoped the fake enthusiasm was good enough.

"I've been into a few things since the good old days," Jackie lied.

Jesus Christ, good old days is right, he thought. *How does a guy like me peak at seventeen and fall so fast that I'm shit-scared of being exposed to a guy I never hung out with?*

"What about you, Petey?"

"Oh, let's see," Ramos replied, "I went into the Marines after school. Big fucking mistake."

Jackie was grateful he wasn't asked to explain his own lousy life since his school days.

"Two Moscow Mules," Ramos told the bartender. Ramos tossed a pair of fifties onto the bar.

He grinned at Jackie as if he'd just performed a complex magic act.

Jackie remembered little about Peter Ramos. Ramos didn't hang with brainiacs, jocks, nerds, or dopers. Not exactly a loner but if you blinked, you'd miss him. Now he looked bulked up, the way his deltoids bunched under the nylon jacket.

Jackie wanted to devour the Moscow Mule in front of him, but he didn't want to look needy. He let Ramos take a sip before he reached out for his.

"Man, I needed that," Pete said. "I tried real estate after the Corps but that fizzled . I did sales for a John Deere outlet. Did that for five years. Shit money but it led me to a man big in agribusiness—you know, hundreds of thousands of acres of soybeans. Filthy rich bastard but more money than brains. He helped me connect. I haven't looked back since."

"Sounds fantastic, Pete."

"I insure farmers against crop damage—you know, hail, rain, insect damage. Most of what I do is consultation. Developing and instituting strategies."

"You sound like a stock broker," Jackie said.

"Ha, it's a lot like that—only riskier than the market. I hold these millionaire farmers' hands and explain to them how to maximize financial gains. It gets any better, I'm going to need a marketing supervisor."

Jackie worried the Big Shot Ramos had become would expect him to buy the next round. He needn't have worried. The fifties were replaced by an identical pair. The loose bills on the bar went into the thongs of the dancers. He and Ramos were surrounded by the hottest girls in the Den, each vying for attention. Jackie's legs and back were nudged and caressed by hands and hips hovering around them, all that sweet flesh on display. The weightlifting lug of a bouncer kept his distance as the girls crowded them like piranhas in a feeding frenzy. The No Touching the Dancers rule suspended whenever big money was flashed.

By closing time, Ramos had treated them both to fifty-dollar lap dances in the back. He was so drunk his girl's sinuous movements and serious face reminded him of a hooded cobra gazing down at a field mouse. The air popped with static electricity. Ramos' girl was swinging her thick buttery hair back and forth across his thighs like a horse's tail shooing flies.

Out in the parking lot was a different scene. The fuggy air of the club with its alcohol fumes, sweat, and perfume was replace by a brittle wind that hit him like a fist in the forehead. He loped drunkenly as far as the rear bumper of his car before his stomach heaved up the witches' brew in his stomach.

Ramos stagger-walked over to him.

"I'm juss—just fine," Jackie blubbered, wiping vomit from his chin with his sleeve.

"You're too wasted to drive, Jackie! Cops'll lock you up for ninety years, they catch you."

"No, no," Jackie replied, throwing a stiff arm out. "I'm good, I'm good."

Jackie had fallen far but not so far he'd let himself be driven home; besides, he didn't want Ramos to see his shithole apartment.

"OK, Jackie boy, take 'er easy. Until we meet again," Ramos said and turned on his heel. The keys in Jackie's hands turned into a bunch of tiny, squirming fish. Across the lot, Jackie watched Ramos get into a cobalt-blue Cayman sitting beneath a cone of light.

Envy washed over him, not for the first time that night. Jackie smacked the steering wheel of his Civic. He hoped Ramos didn't notice.

Jackie's foul, vomitous breath rolled back from the windshield to assault his nose. "God damn it to hell, that punk kid at work called it. 'Freeloader.' I'm a loser."

He made it back to his apartment without drawing attention of cops like a wounded gazelle limping through the savanna, hoping the lions are sleeping.

The next day's hangover was a beauty. Jackie had a vague memory of his cell ringing around seven. *Work*, he figured. *Screw that*.

Around midday, he felt human enough to stagger into the tiny kitchen and make coffee. He took a chance on plain toast and lost. The toilet bowl caught the remnants of his stomach just in time. The stench was godawful.

Close to four, he had his bearings again despite the dizziness that occurred if he moved too abruptly. He was a long way from an appetite but he could think of food without the urge to upchuck.

The phone rang at five. This time, he intercepted it before that smartass at the construction site could fire him.

"Yo, Jack, you there? C'mon, Cash Money, pick up. It's me, your old drinking buddy."

Ramos crooned a couple ffkey the Badger fight song from those stupid pep rallies.

"Hey, Pete. I'm here," Jackie replied.

"How you feeling boy?"

"Like hammered shit, like an asshole casserole. Like somebody stomped out my brains and took a shit in my mouth. Like—"

"I get it, I get it, man. Me, too. I haven't drunk like that since my first furlough from boot camp," Ramos said.

Jackie thought: *You never drank like that, Pete.*

"What's up, Pete?"

"I need you to do me a little favor," Pete said.

Fuck me, here it comes. Payback for last night's free booze and pussy rubdown.

93

"Look," Pete said, a new note of concern in his voice, "can we meet somewhere? I don't want to talk about this on the phone."

Jackie hesitated. He almost said: *Pete, I'm a brokedick dog, I got nothing, I can't help you, man.*

Instead he replied, "Sure, Pete, wherever. Name it."

Jackie knew the restaurant Pete named. It was an expensive seafood restaurant in the Warehouse District, far from the homeless drifters and inner-city thugs like the Heartless Felons roaming around for easy prey—those low-level office workers in the high-rises who stopped for one drink too many before fleeing the dangerous city to their cozy nests in suburbia.

"Hey, wear a suit," Ramos had said before ending the connection.

Jackie had last worn a suit and tie when his opioid-addicted mother bit the Big One after a fentanyl overdose. He felt he wasn't altogether sober yet. He'd awakened in a greasy sweat from a recurring nightmare—being chased through a golden meadow that turned into a slurry of muck the color of baby shit. The chaser carried a weapon—an axe? A sword? He couldn't remember the details. He just knew he woke up shit-scared.

Jackie's education was basically zilch before and after high school. He used to brag in the bars he never read a book in four years. Now, looking through his stained window at the part of downtown the Chamber of Commerce didn't want tourists to see, he wondered if he ought to have cracked open a book on interpreting dreams by that guy the TV shrinks yakked about.

*

94

"You believe it?" he said as they were led to their table, "my whole life in this burgh and my first time here."

"We'll toast to 'first times,'" Ramos said. He flicked a couple fingers at the sommelier already heading their way.

Jackie was impressed by the *grandeur* on display: waiters in crisp tuxedoes, black shoes shined to mirror polish, the sommelier with his silver cup on a gold chain, the beefeater out front who looked like some guy who got out of the wrong taxi and missed the curtain call for the Shakespeare play in Public Square.

Jackie deferred to Ramos at ordering their fare. He also chose the wine.

"What's that tiny silver cup for on the chain?"

"That's a 'tastevin,'" Ramos replied. "It's more for show nowadays. Before electricity, you could check the clarity and color of wine better than in a glass down in a darkened wine cellar."

"I see," Jackie said. He didn't.

"Look, Pete, I need to say something. I don't know what the bill for this feast will come to, but I am flat-assed broke. But I can pay you back—"

"Forget it, man" Ramos said; "my treat. I was a little down when I walked into the Cougar's Nest or Coyote Heaven or whatever that bar's called, and you cheered me up. I'm just repaying the favor you did me."

That dog didn't hunt, but Jackie said nothing, grateful to be let off the hook. Ramos and the blues didn't go together with fifties flying out of his wallet like toilet tissue, never mind the $80,000 Porsche. Jackie's shaggy memory from the bender was yielding to reality; he knew the difference between somebody pissing on his leg and rain.

"Oh yeah?"

"About the money," Ramos said, "You can help me out of a little jam I got myself into."

"I haven't got two nickels to rub together," Jackie replied. "I just lost the only job I've had in weeks—"

"No, no, no, it's not about money," Ramos interjected. "Look, let's enjoy the grilled sea bass and the scallops. They're as big as pig's knuckles here. By the way, did you know sea bass isn't actually bass? Yeah, it's Patagonian Toothfish. Some marketing wizard thought 'Chilean sea bass' sounded more like something Americans would go for . . ."

Jackie half-listened. The snobbery wasn't the thing bugging him. Ramos worked too hard with his forced friendliness. Jackie knew he was born; he just wasn't born yesterday, he wanted to say.

" . . . so I'll be in Wichita all weekend talking to some farmers about crop productivity technologies. I can't afford not to be there, Jackie. Can you help a brother, do me a solid?"

The wheedling finally put a cap on it, the whole "help a brother out" *shtik* Ramos had been dinning in his ear throughout the liqueur and crème brûlée. Trying to be casual about it but Jackie could see the narrowed eyes and the focus behind the words.

But it didn't sound like much of a favor, come down to it, and, what the hell, Ramos was willing to pay five hundred dollars just for impersonating him over the weekend. *Use my credit card, order up all the pizza and beer you want . . .*

Compared to shoveling construction debris into a "shit chute" three stories down to the dumpster, this sounded like a piece of cake. *So what if he's playing me*, Jackie thought.

"I'll do it," Jackie said.

Ramos, all teeth, toasted him with his fancy wine glass.

*

The tricky part was going into public as "Peter Ramos." *Wear the hoodie, keep the drawstrings tight around the face, don't stare into anybody's eyes . . .*

Jackie was the same height but gave away thirty pounds. That gap was accommodated by a quilted vest under the hoodie. He spotted the teller he was supposed to look for at the end. He had to step out of line twice, pretending to make out a deposit slip. The bank's closed-circuit cameras were the most expensive and boasted high-pixel-definition.

No shit, Captain Obvious, Ramos sneered; that's why you don't stare at the lenses . . .

Jackie timed it just right. He stepped up to MaryBeth Atjemis' screened window. *Dumber than a bag of dicks*, Ramos had said. *She wouldn't recognize anybody at the Last Supper with their halos on.* Still, he wiped away a sheen of perspiration on his forehead during the simple transaction. *You say two words exactly, 'Deposit, please,' and grunt if she starts talking about the weather or her period, whatever. Stand in profile, look at your shoes, but do NOT look up . . .*

He'd spent the rest of the weekend in Ramos' plush apartment in the Flats by the river, snarfing pizzas paid online with Ramos' credit card, adding generous tips for the drivers, downing Jack, chasing it with beer, and soaking in a sauna-sized bathtub with a keypad thermal readout.

Ramos' answering machine recorded messages that sounded like business. If he had

97

to answer, Jackie was told, he was to cough and muffle his voice, say he had a head cold and wouldn't be in until Monday afternoon.

Not a bad way to make five hundred bones, all in all. And all because the guy had "a fantastic business" opportunity, that, if it panned out, Ramos bragged, would set him in an exclusive deal for life, one he didn't intend to bring his partner in on—"I'll get sued later by the prick, but I'll worry about that later, right, Jackie, boy? Boning a new girlfriend on the side was "a bonus."

"What if your girlfriend shows up?" Jackie asked.

"She won't," Ramos said, "but if she does, you can fuck her."

Some guys have all the luck, as the Rod Stewart tune went.

*

Ramos wanted to meet in the parking lot of the Coyote Den for "the payoff."

"Why not the bar?" Jackie asked. "Have a drink to celebrate your victory—if that's what it was."

"What do you mean by that?"

Ramos' tone dropped to Arctic chill.

"Nothing, man," Jackie said.

"Can't," Ramos pleaded, "I've got a massive amount of work to catch up on. I can't wait to get free of that slave-driving prick of a partner."

Again, working too hard to convince. Ramos had not said a single word about even having a partner when they met up the first time at the Den. Now the partner's the spawn of Satan.

"No problem."

Jackie returned to his stool at the bar; several pairs of eyes met his. He slapped the first hundred on the bar top, exclaiming, "Drinks on me!"

Four hours later, he was broke again. Between the barflies and the dancers, he was cored like an apple.

Joey the bartender and the bouncer each gripped a bicep and led him out to his car.

"Jack, you need to cool it down some," Joey told him; the bouncer fished in his Jackie's pockets for the keys.

"We can't let him drive like this," Joey said, propping him against the side of the Civic.

"Fuck him," the bouncer said. "I didn't get none of that cash he was throwin' around like confetti."

*

Three days later, Jackie was back in the welfare office sitting on a bench with dozens of others with a sticky number card in his hand waiting for his turn to be called to see a caseworker. A black woman with a squalling baby and a toddler left her *Plain Dealer* on the same bench and dragged her toddler off to the restroom. Jackie scooted over to fetch the paper. Something to occupy his mind while he waited.

A subheading below the fold caught his eye: *Woman Abducted from Home and Found Murdered in Woods.*

Jackie was about to turn the page when a couple phrases jumped out of the column and nearly gagged him: " . . . divorced from her husband . . . Peter Ramos, entrepreneur and resident of the city . . ."

Jackie staggered out of the hallway, gripped the banister rail tight and took the steps down to the foyer out through the revolving doors into pedestrian traffic on Ninth Street. He zig-zagged like a drunk stumbling into traffic.

He slapped his pockets for his cell phone. He punched the number Ramos gave him.

"What the fuck did you do, motherfucker!" Jackie screamed, oblivious of the passersby suddenly splitting in two like a bow wave.

"Me, I didn't do anything, Jackie. But you did," Ramos calmly replied. "Don't say anything stupid when the cops come calling."

"What—"

The call was abruptly terminated by Ramos' thumb at the other end.

Mother of God, he was more than an alibi. He was accessory to murder.

*

. . . . when the cops come calling . . .

Jackie couldn't get the words out of his brain. But they didn't—not for two long days. By then, he'd worn a path in the tiny apartment's shitty brown rug.

He told the big detective whose name was "Franks" or something like that "of course he'd be happy" to come down to the station and make a statement "about his friendship with Mister Peter Ramos."

Happy? Oh fuck me . . .

He spent a sleepless night considering his options including fleeing town but finally made up his mind between showering and dressing.

He told the two cops behind the big, scarred desk in the detective bureau everything he remembered about meeting Ramos in the Coyote Den that night and the dinner at the restaurant later—but not word one about impersonating Ramos the weekend Ramos' wife was murdered in her parents' home in Monroe, Michigan. He

100

thought of the big cop as "Frankenstein" and the little one as "Igor."

Looking from one to the other, a mouse caught between a pair of cat claws, he hoped they were buying it, but they looked like a pair of cigar-store Indians, no giveaway expressions, just one question after another. Did he think it odd that Ramos and he got together like that? Did he know Ramos was going to lose big in a divorce settlement? On and on it went.

"CCTV from the bars in the Flats was out of range," Frankenstein said, "but one camera shows Mister Ramos in his doorway picking up the pizza from the driver."

Jackie waited for the other shoe to drop.

"Trouble is," Igor said, "it don't look much like Ramos. The FBI is cleaning up the video."

"Yeah," Frankenstein chimes in, "the got the same computers NASA uses."

"I see," Jackie said. He figured anybody sitting in the hot seat like him would ask it.

"Who is it?"

Frankenstein answered, "It looks like you, Mister Frielander."

"I don't know how that could be," Jackie replied, and tried to look appropriately stupefied. *Jesus, fuck, I'm sweating . . . they can see me sweating . . .*

The look of astonishment froze on his face, an innocent man's expression—he hoped.

"That's right," Igor said, leaning toward him. "Can you explain that?"

"No, sir."

Three hours of being grilled. By the time he left them, dragging along their veiled threat they'd be back with more questions, he was limp with exhaustion.

Back in his dingy apartment, he closed the blinds and pulled the phone jack out of the wall. He killed the half-bottle of Old Ezra kept in the cupboard "for emergencies." An hour later, he collapsed on his bed. Real sirens in the streets punctuated his nightmare of being chased into a tunnel with one end blocked. The smeary light of dawn slipped around the ripped Venetian blinds and smacked him in both eyeballs.

Jackie set up in bed. He stared at the cracks in the walls that looked like pieces of a giant puzzle crudely put together. "I'm not his patsy," he said aloud, "I'm his only loose end."

Everybody knows what happens to loose ends.

Jackie dressed fast, shoving clothing aside, tossing clothing over his shoulders like Walmart shoppers at a discount bin on Black Friday. He found his stash he'd forced himself to squirrel away no matter how desperate he got. He counted the total—five-hundred. *Jesus,* he prayed, *be enough.* He hit the streets without bothering with coffee first.

One advantage to being poor as a shithouse mouse was that you met "interesting" people, many living on society's rawer edge. He knew a couple among the pack who might be able to help him, the kind who'd never ask questions, and if cops did come calling, they'd make themselves as scarce as fleas on an eel.

*

He heard a whisper as he staggered into the bedroom.

"Tied another one on," the voice said from the darkened corner. "You really are a worthless piece of shit."

102

Jackie turned around to face the corner where Ramos' voice came from. A pencil of light above his head was the only indication of the man's presence in the room.

"Don't shoot me," Jackie begged.

"Stop whining, loser, and man up. Face it, deep down, you had to know this was coming."

Ramos' voice grew huskier, the adrenalin hitting his blood stream—*Getting ready to commit another murder*, Jackie knew.

"Why kill me?" Jackie pleaded.

"Can you be that dumb?" Ramos said. "The cops can't break me. They know it. My alibi's air-tight thanks to you. But you—well, that's another thing altogether, right?"

The sound of Ramos' laugh issued from the hole in his face in that invisible space a few feet from where Jackie stood rooted to the floor.

"Nice pigsty you got here, by the way," Ramos mocked. He made a different sound like someone gagging on a fish bone.

Playing with me, a cat with a mouse . . .

"I won't break, Pete, I swear it!"

"Oh, you'll break, all right, 'Freeloader'—that's how I found you that night. The bartender at that skank tittie bar told me they call you that behind your back. 'Cash Money,' my ass. A long time ago, eh, Jackie? But before I send you off to your reward, I want you to know you played a valuable part in my life, and I'm ever so grateful—"

The sound of gunfire in the small apartment was louder than he'd anticipated. One of the bullets made a ferocious ricochet. Jackie figured one of his shots must have dinged off the metal hinge of the door behind Ramos' head.

His ears rang from squeezing off so many rounds in so small a space. Ramos' arrogant voice acted like a beacon for Jackie to place his shots. He never heard the body drop to the floorboards. The air in the room stank with an acrid bite from unloading half a clip.

He hit the light switch and saw the crumpled form of Pete Ramos, legs tucked under him like a sleeping alley bum. The small-caliber gun he'd brought with its tube silencer was lying in his lap, a hand folded over the butt. Jackie saw the tiny red hole just above Ramos' left eyebrow, a lucky shot. Ramos had come dressed—all black from his military boots to the matte-black hoodie spattered with blood.

He tried sorting out the different emotions roiling within while he patted his pants pocket for the business card Det. Frankenstein gave him the day he left headquarters downtown.

. . . my card with the number if you think of anything to add to your statement, the big cop had said.

Then he remembered tossing it into a trash receptacle in the lobby of the police building. Jackie figured he'd have a little time to collect his thoughts before the cops arrived. He surprised himself to discover he wasn't as afraid of the jail time ahead as he'd feared when he felt Frankenstein's and Igor's stares lasering his back as he left their office.

He felt suddenly oxygen-deprived, giddy, an actor after an exhausting stage performance— nerveshot from pretending to be sloshed every night coming home to his place, wondering if this was the night Ramos would be waiting in ambush . . .

The nine-one-one dispatcher told him officers were on their way, shots had been reported coming from his building; he hung up despite the fact she told him to stay on the line.

He stepped over to the corpse, hunching low to stare at the dead man on his floor.

"You talked too much at the restaurant, Pete," Jackie told the body. "I knew you wouldn't shoot me straight away. You like to brag. How's it feel now?"

The sirens shredding the air out in the street made him jump up. Alternating splashes of crimson and turquoise light bounced off the ceiling and walls. In seconds, his whole apartment block was shrouded in the bright lights of police cruisers converging on his apartment block.

Jackie stood up, walked into his living room with his street purchase, a .9 mm Hi-Point with its serial numbers filed away, dangling loosely from his hand. He wondered what he was going to do when the pounding on his door began.

***

©2019 Robb T. White

WHAT PRICE WOULD YOU PAY
TO SAVE YOUR FAMILY

AMANDA
DONOHOE

OM
PURI

VITHAYA
PANSRINGARM

GUY RATCHANONT
SUPRAKOB

JONATHAN
RAGGETT

TRAFFICKER

A FILM BY LARRY SMITH

QUICK & DIRTY

FLASH ⚡ FICTION FICTION ⚡ FICTION

FLASH ⚡ FICTION SH ⚡ FICTION

FI SH ⚡ FICTION

SH ⚡ FICTION

SH ⚡ FICTION

SH ⚡ FICTION

SH ⚡ FICTION

A Brand New Outfit

Jim G. Wilsky

Slow and easy, Salvatore Alimonte came down the basement steps of his vacation house in rural Wisconsin. He was in amazingly good shape for being seventy-five, and just as important, for all the hard living he'd done over so many years. All that said, his right knee had been hurting like a bitch for about a week now. Other than the bum knee though, Big Sal looked and felt like a million bucks.

He was dressed in a grey suit jacket, light blue dress shirt that was open at the collar and no tie. Charcoal grey slacks and black Berluti loafers finished off the look. He was tanned, like always, still fit and trim. When and if he smiled, his teeth were so white they'd blind you. Against all tradition, he'd always hated bling. No gold necklace chains or loopy gold bracelets and heavy rings. He didn't even like watches.

He stopped about three steps from the bottom, panned the softly lit finished basement and took a drag of his cigarette. Faces seated around the table looked at him silently. Sal took a sip of his bourbon and said, "Alright, we ate, we had some drinks. Now we get to business."

The longtime consigliere, Albert Vitale started making his way down from the kitchen too. His steps on the wooden stairway echoed in the stillness.

Sal flashed a joking smile, "While you fuckin' jagoffs been yucking it up down here, Allie and I been talking upstairs. I got a few things to say." He held the smile but his eyes, his eyes told the real story.

The Capos seated around the large circular table were solemn and serious, except for Johnny

Palmisano, who had stood up to greet the reappearance of his boss like the ass kisser he was. "Johnny P" who had Chinatown, also had a big stupid grin on his face but as Sal's dark eyes floated around and finally settled on him, that smile began to melt away. Palmisano eased himself back down in his chair.

This was the Big Sal from back in the day. Setting you up with a little joke before the storm. You just had to ride it out and see what was going to happen. Palmisano was forty-nine and the youngest guy at the table, but the dumbass should have known better. The other three Capos did. They hadn't seen it for a long time, but they knew and remembered. They were also pretty sure of it now.

Cosimo Bocca, who had Cicero, was sitting between Palmisano and Carmine Pacelli from Grand Ave. After too many drinks one night with Pacelli, Bocca had said it best, "Big Sal, yeah. Yeah, he's like the lion in those news stories you hear. Like at the Lincoln Park Zoo or somethin'. You know, there's a handler that raised this lion from a cub. For seven, eight years maybe, the same guy feeds him. Same guy takes care of him…all a that shit. Lion fuckin' loves him. Then one day, right out of the blue…the dog whistle blows. Handler gets chewed to pieces by that lion. I mean, by the time they can tranquilize him, the fuckin' cat is already gnawing on a shin bone like it's a chew stick."

Vitale sat down at the table next to Joe Pascal from Elmwood Park, but Big Sal remained standing and he leaned over to stab his cigarette out in an ashtray. He looked around the table at all of them before straightening back up. "Anybody got anything to say before I start?"

He waited a full, silent minute then held up his forefinger. "Okay look, I got three fuckin' things that are just eatin' at my gut…and I'm gonna fix all three tonight. Number one, since Anthony got pinched in March, I been without an underboss."

Sal held up two fingers and his voice got louder, "Two, our numbers are way the fuck down. We been hunkered down for too long. Laying low is one thing, laying down is another. We're too soft. Somebody is late paying taxes, we let them stall us. Somebody gets pressured on the price for a shipment of Horse, we settle. Some fuckin' guy in Melrose Park that needs his legs broke, we just bitch slap him instead."

"Fucking Three", He was yelling now. "Word is, somebody is getting ready to flip."

If there had been a clock in the room, you could've heard it ticking.

Big Sal stopped pacing, drained his tumbler and slammed it on the table. The veins in his neck were standing out and his eyes were blazing now. A lock of his silver hair was out of place, curling down on his forehead.

"So, enough is enough", he said and started walking around the table. Big Sal reached Bocca and then put a hand on his shoulder.

Bocca had a blank look that betrayed nothing. He took a casual sip of his beer and sat it down. Anyone who doubted his brass balls, didn't anymore.

"The guy that's gonna flip", Sal looked around at the rest of them, "ain't this fucking guy. He's standup, my top earner and he's the new acting underboss. Cosimo is gonna solve number one and help you fix number two. Allie, get him a bourbon from the bar." Sal started clapping and the rest were quick to join in. Grins and laughs were all around the table.

Albert Vitale got up and walked to the mini bar on the side wall. He had tried to talk Sal out of this next part. Number three. He'd told Sal it was Palmisano but warned him not here, and more importantly, not to do it himself.

He poured slow, hoping Sal would come to his senses.

The table was still chattering with laughs and congratulations when Sal said from behind Vitale, "Jesus your slow, gimme Cosimo's drink."

Vitale turned and he dropped the drink, just a second before being shot just above his left eye.

Big Sal Alimonte aimed downward and put another round into the back of Vitale's head.

He took the bottle of bourbon, walked back to the table of men and said, "Number three. Solved."

There was only a short delay before the back slapping and celebrating came back to the group. Just as Sal knew it would. Afterall, there's nothing worse than a snitch…and there's a certain relief. Plus, fuck it, there was a new job opening for some lucky bastard.

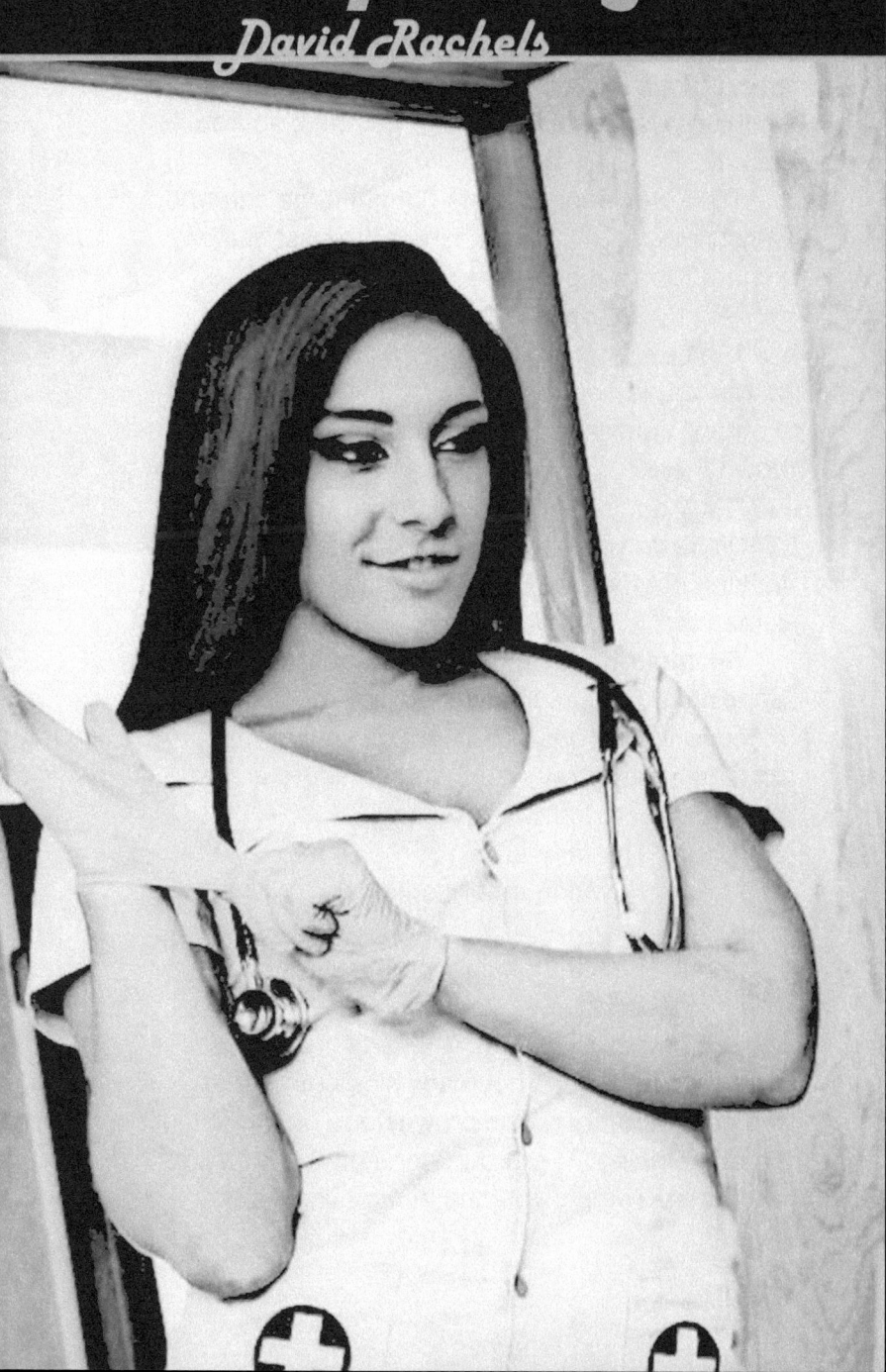

The Lady Urologist

David Rachels

I'm complaining again about how my piss burns when Seymour asks me if I've got the clap.

I say, "Not unless you can get the clap from your fist."

Then Seymour tells me I ought to go see "the lady urologist." He says, "She's the best in the tristate. She's a burn specialist."

"A *lady* urologist?"

"She's a doctor. Doctors specialize. Cockrell wants you to see the best, and the best is a woman. You want some quack working on you down there?"

"How does the boss know? Did you tell him?"

"Why do you care how he knows? He's looking out for you. She's expecting you tomorrow."

Seymour hands me one of those little appointment cards like you get at a doctor's office, only this one hasn't got much information on it, just tomorrow's date and an address.

"Do I get to know her name?"

"Who? The lady urologist?"

"Yeah. How come her name's not on the card?"

"Well, she's the best in the tristate, so what do you care? Cockrell says go, you go."

So the next day, I go. The lady urologist's brownstone doesn't have any signs other than the house number. The brownstone on the left is an obstetrician. The brownstone on the right is a podiatrist. The brownstone in the middle doesn't have a sign. Why doesn't the lady urologist have a sign? I'm concerned. Suspicious, even. I've felt this way all along, but if I skip this appointment, Cockrell will know, and that could be bad for me. Also, the burn is getting worse, so yeah, I need to see a doctor. Time to go inside.

The brownstone's doorknob doesn't turn, and I almost walk into the door. Why would the door be locked? I look at the appointment card again to check the address. Then I notice there *is* one small sign, right below the doorbell: SONNEZ SVP. So at least now I know the doctor's name. I don't know about the SVP, but I figure it must be doctor-speak for urologist.

I ring the bell.

The door opens like someone had been waiting on the other side. A woman leans out and looks at me.

"Dr. Sonnez?" I say.

"Mr. Keaton?" she says.

"That's me."

"Entrez," she says. She leans back into the brownstone and opens the door wide.

I go inside, and it doesn't look like a doctor's office. I'm standing at the front of someone's living room.

"It's an unconventional arrangement," Dr. Sonnez says. "I live downstairs, work upstairs, and you can only get there from here."

I get my first good look at her. She's older than me, an attractive brunette, but with her hair pulled back and her makeup subdued. She's working hard to look professional, but she's wearing a business suit. She looks like she belongs in a board room, not an examination room.

"Follow me," she says, and she heads to the stairs on our left. As we go up, I try not to stare at her ass, but there it is, so what am I supposed to do? When we get to the top of the stairs, the hallway still looks like somebody's house, not a doctor's office. We pass an open bathroom door, and I can see a cat's litter box inside. "Right in here," she says, and we go into the first door past the bathroom. "Have a seat on the table."

The table is silver metal without any kind of covering. There's a sink, but I don't see any soap. There's a folding chair. There's a low bookcase with issues of *National Geographic* and *Reader's Digest*. And that's all. I sit on the silver table. It's so cold, I can feel it through my pants.

I say, "Do you need me to fill out any forms? Medical history and all that?"

"Not necessary," says Dr. Sonnez. "Mr. Cockrell has taken care of that."

I say, "Cockrell knows my medical history?"

Dr. Sonnez ignores that. She says, "Take off your pants and underwear, and I'll be right back."

She leaves the room. I climb down from the table and strip below the waist. There's no way I'm putting my bare ass on that freezing metal, so I just stand there, waiting, feeling exposed. I have to take a piss.

She comes back carrying a bunch of rubber tubing attached to something that looks like a bicycle pump.

I say, "I've got to take a leak. Is that good timing? So you can see the problem in action?"

"Perfect timing," says the doctor. "I was going to catheterize you in any event, but now I can really see what's going on. Get back on the table."

I get back on the table, forgetting how cold it's going to be. I yell.

"Are you warming up?" she says, and while I'm trying to figure out what she means by that, she tells me to lie down. As I'm raising my feet onto the table, she puts her hand on my shoulder and pushes me over backwards. She says, "Do you want lubricant?"

I say, "Is that a joke?"

She says, "Lubricant it is," and a moment later, I feel it. I expect it to hurt, but it doesn't hurt. It just feels strange. It feels like I'm pissing in reverse.

"All right, now," says Dr. Sonnez. "There are certain things that Mr. Cockrell wants to know about what went wrong with the Feldman heist. You'll tell me the truth, or I'll use this catheter."

My impulse is to run, but there's a tube coming out of my dick attached to the bicycle-pump-looking-thing in her hand. I say, "Use the catheter how?"

She says, "This is a one-of-a-kind candiru catheter. I designed it myself."

117

I say, "Candiru?"

She says, "It's a kind of fish. A very special kind of fish. Do you know about the candiru's special talent?"

"No," I say, "what's the candiru's special talent?"

She says, "It's easier if I just show you."

***

©2019 David Rachels

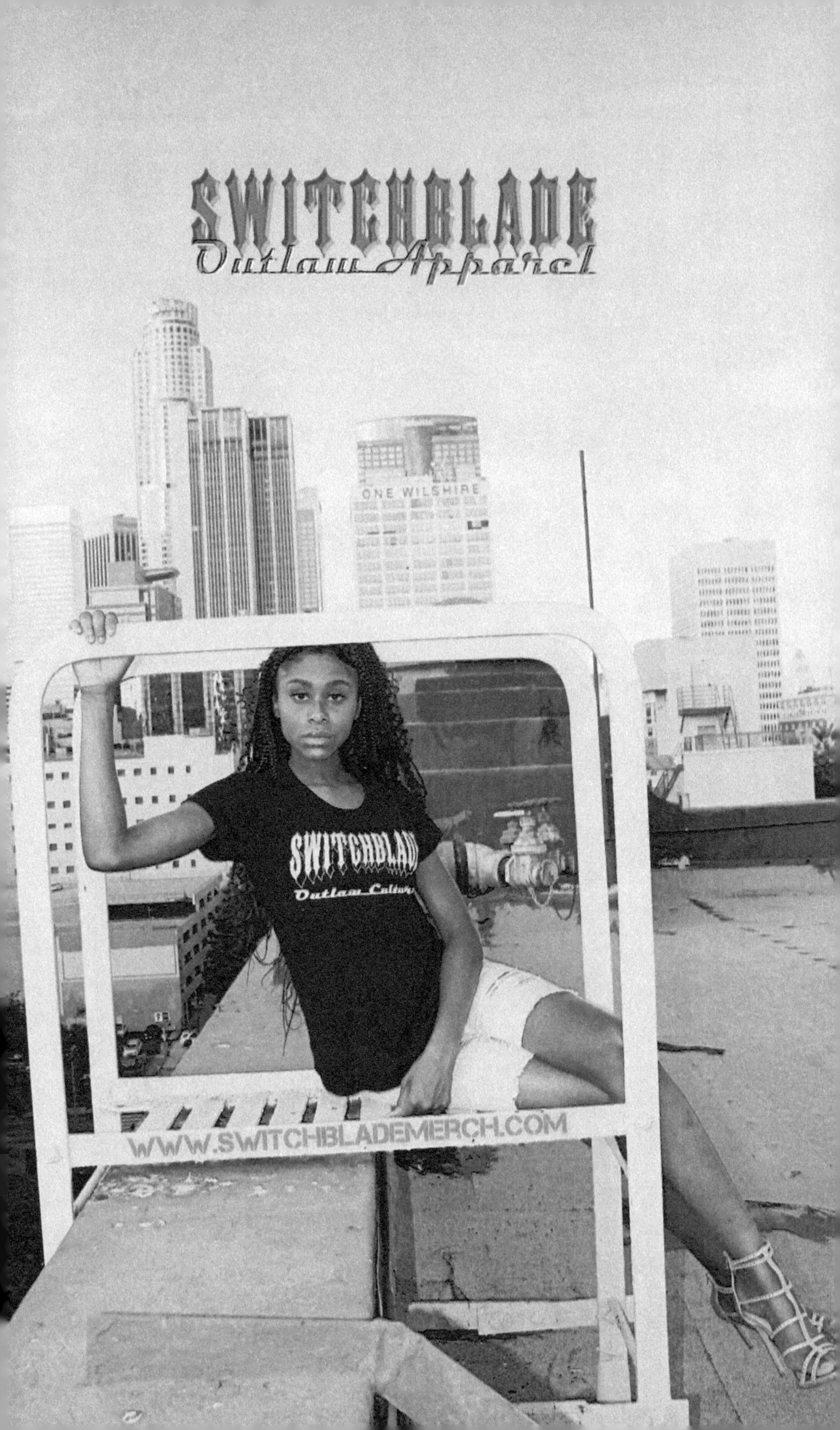
SWITCHBLADE
Outlaw Apparel
ONE WILSHIRE
SWITCHBLADE
Outlaw Culture
WWW.SWITCHBLADEMERCH.COM

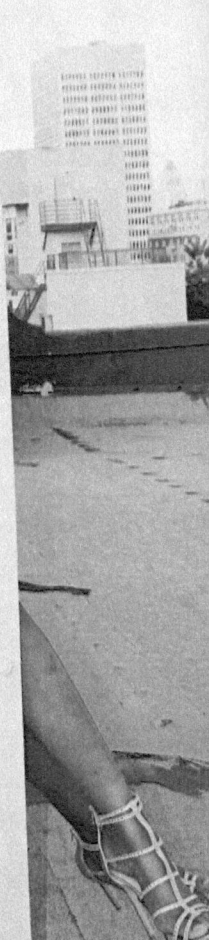

AN ANTHOLOGY OF NOIR

SWITCHBLADE

ISSUE TEN

TIMOTHY FRIEND
JIM TOWNS
SERENA JAYNE
TIM V. DECKER
CHRISTIAN GOSS
JIM WILSKY
NW BARCUS
GENE BREAZNELL
BEAUMONT RAND
EDDIE MCNAMARA
CW BLACKWELL

SWITCHBLADE
PERSON OF INTEREST

Name: Alec Cizak

Birthplace: Indianapolis, IN

First Appearance: SB Issue 5

Appearances: SB Issue 5,
SB Issue 11

Alec Cizak is a pillar of the independent pulp community.

Alec Cizak is a writer, publisher, and a filmmaker. His work has appeared in several journals and anthologies. His most recent novel, "Breaking Glass", is available from ABC Group Documentation. He is the editor of the fiction journal, Pulp Modern. He has a forthcoming short story collection release, slotted for October, called "Lake County Incidents", also from ABC Documentation. According to Cizak, 'it's a macabre collection of stories set around fictitious small towns near Gary, IN.' Also forthcoming from Mr. Cizak, is the Pulp Modern release of "Tech Noir", a team up set of special issues from both Switchblade and Pulp Modern.

Switchblade caught up with Mr.Cizak, and got a slice of the man's cutting edge wisdom

Who are you, where are you from, and how long have you been writing?

I'm Alec Cizak. I come from the geographic center of the universe, Indianapolis, Indiana. I've been writing my entire life. I wrote my first story in the fourth grade. It was about a scientist who trains a tree to rob banks. Obviously, I was an environmentally-conscious crime fiction author before it was trendy. Nothing I wrote, however, was particularly good until I got into my late 30s/early 40s. You have to live quite a while before you have anything relevant to say about the human condition.

What makes a great story?

A great story finds a way to capture a reader's attention and holds it with great prose. That's all there is to it. And, of course, it's the most complicated thing in the world. A great story will usually challenge a reader's world view (a tough thing to do in the age of "safe spaces," but it is the writer's responsibility to do so regardless of the whims of the zeitgeist, for literature lasts longer than trends). And, to be honest, a great story will honor mythic form. Experimental fiction is interesting for a paragraph or so, but the human mind will eventually reject it. And, frankly, the great "experiments" have already been done (Finnegan's Wake, Tropic of Cancer, Naked Lunch, Lost in the Funhouse, etc.). We're in the punk rock stage of literature, meaning, going back to the basics and adding some sharp teeth to the proceedings.

Define noir.

Noir celebrates human misery. The noir writer cuts to the chase and says, "Hey, life's a joke and then you die." A good noir story or book, in my opinion, should help the reader understand the loneliness of the individual is a shared experience.

Why do you write in the noir genre?

Well, I prefer to write horror stories, but those are very difficult for me because I don't want to cheat the reader—I don't want to promise the reader a freakout and not deliver. Also, so much modern horror seems contingent on needless gore. I want to write more elegant horror stories. So, short story long, I've been writing mostly crime fiction because it's fairly close to the horror genre (think about how many of the crime and horror EC comics stories were interchangeable) and it satisfies my desire to tell stories about people the status quo would otherwise ignore.

Who is the author who most influenced you?

So many writers have influenced me. The writer who liberated my mind, with respect to crime fiction, was Jim Thompson. I'd wanted to write crime fiction for years but couldn't stand the solving-the-mystery aspect. I'm too lazy to do the gobs of research necessary to write crime procedurals (and, frankly,

they bore me anyway). I had read a Ken Bruen book
that quoted Thompson at the beginning of every
chapter so I figured maybe I should read his work.
I found a copy of Pop. 1280 at the old Mystery
Bookstore in Westwood (RIP) and my mind exploded.
It was like I'd been waiting for permission to
write about the degenerates I hung out with when
I was a young idiot in Indianapolis. The thought
just hadn't occurred to me that it was possible
to write about criminals and leave the whole law
 enforcement aspect out of it.

**Who is your favorite author in the independent
crime fiction community?**

I give the same answer every time I'm asked this
question - The greatest "unknown" writer today is
Garnett Elliott. While he works in many different
genres, I first learned about his work through Beat
to a Pulp. He's a master storyteller and he writes
the cleanest prose I've ever read. If pulp fiction
is your thing, you need to be reading this guy's
stories.

The Future is Noir

Pulp Modern

Tech Noir Special   Fall 2019

Tom Barlow • C.W. Blackwell • Deborah L. Davitt
Angelique Fawns • Nils Gilbertson • J.D. Graves
Zakariah Johnson • Jo Perry • Don Stoll

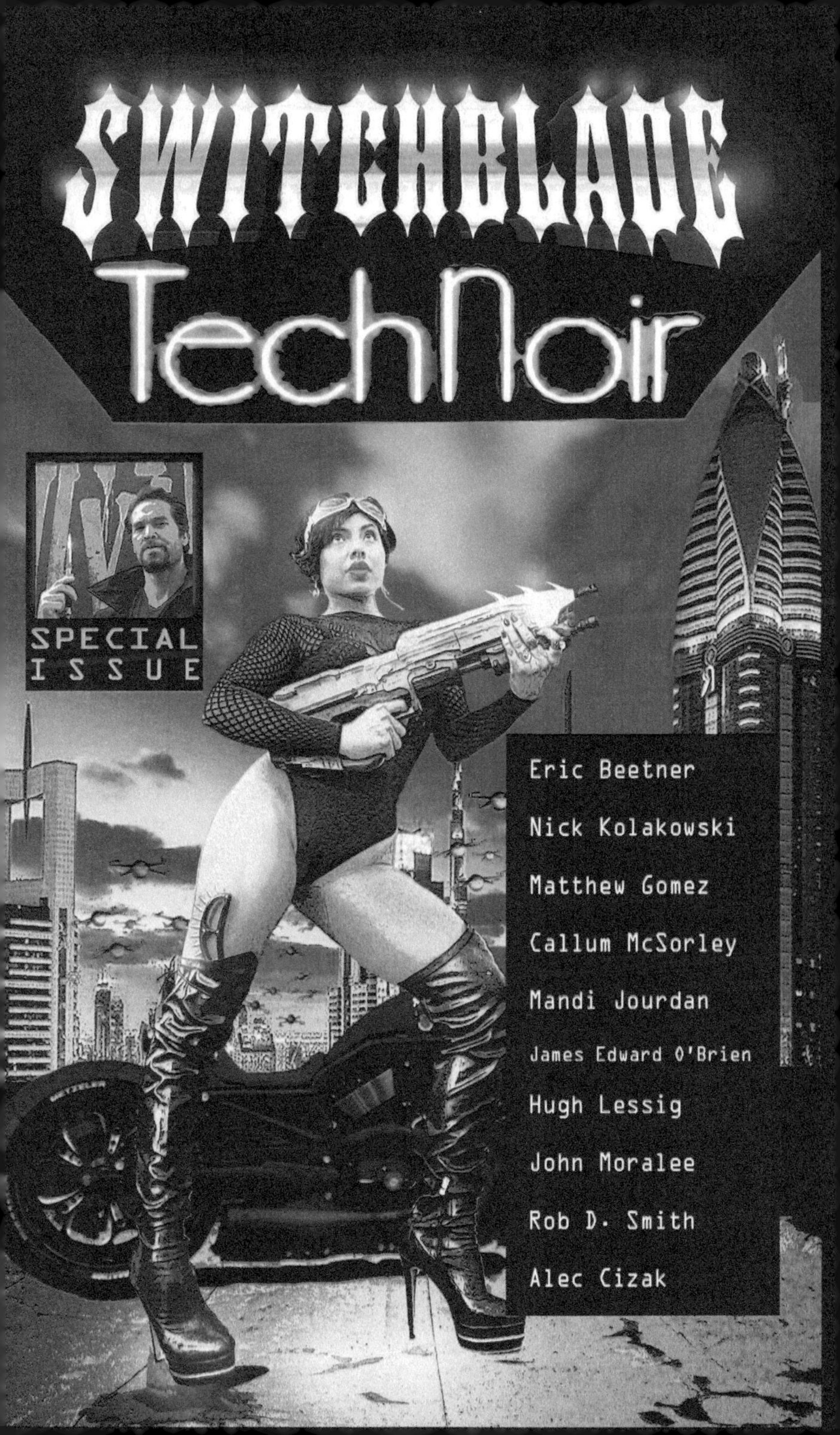
SWITCHBLADE
TechNoir
SPECIAL ISSUE
Eric Beetner
Nick Kolakowski
Matthew Gomez
Callum McSorley
Mandi Jourdan
James Edward O'Brien
Hugh Lessig
John Moralee
Rob D. Smith
Alec Cizak

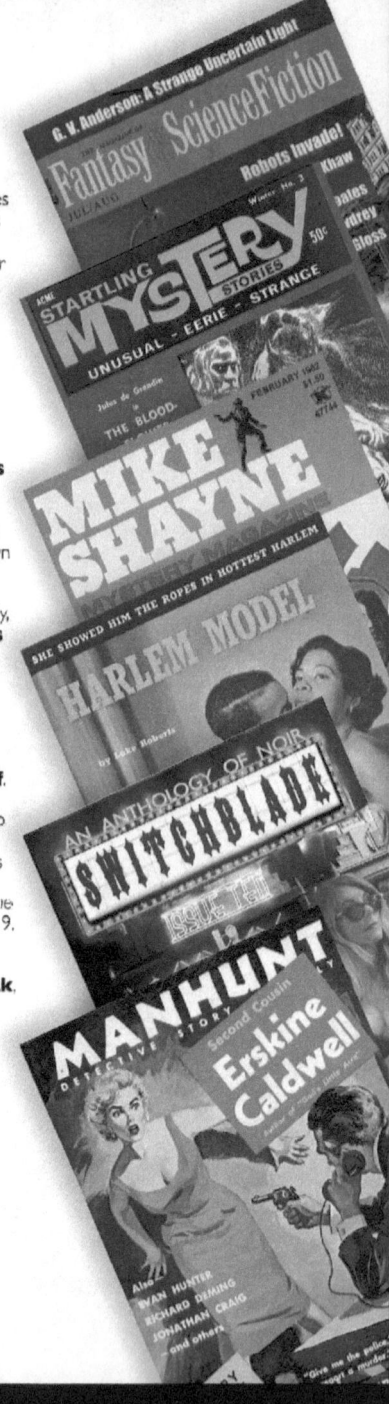

SWITCHBLADE

NOW AVAILABLE AT

DESCONTROL
PUNK SHOP
1725 E 7TH ST #C LOS ANGELES
OPEN EVERY DAY
12-8PM

BUY
DESTROY
SELL
TRADE

(IG) DESCONTROL_SHOP

CLOTHING · LEATHER · ACCESSORIES · RECORDS · TAPES

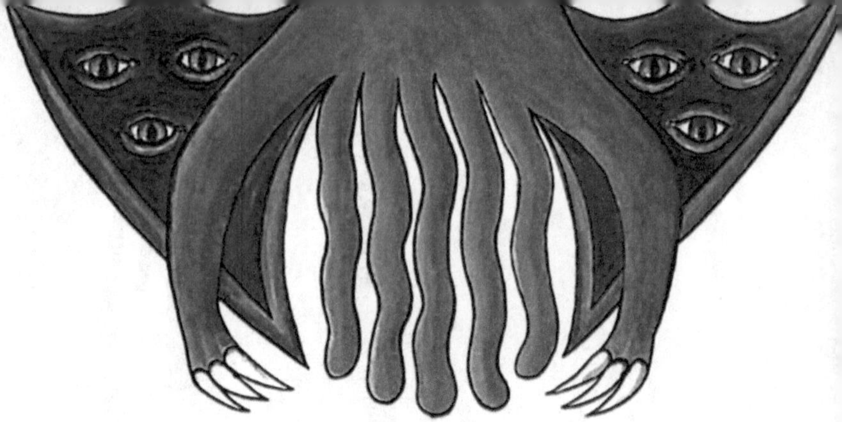

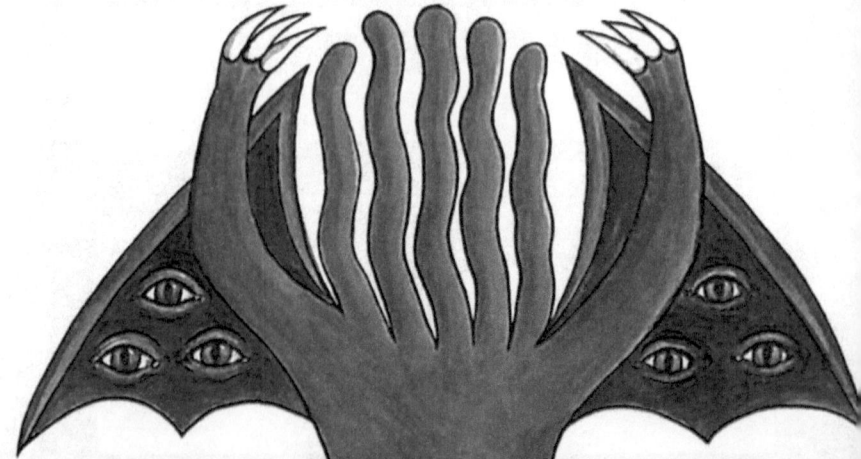

Fresh Pulp Every Wednesday on

New Pulp Tales.com

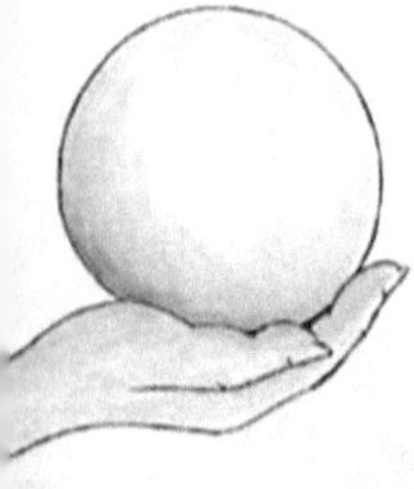

Sword & Sorcery, Weird Tales, Science Fiction, Hard-Boiled Detectives, & Classic Pulp Discussions

INDIE RIGHTS

    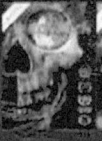   

Author Bios & Acknowledgements

Brian Beatty is the author of the poetry collections *Dust and Stars: Miniatures* (2018, Cholla Needles Press), *Brazil, Indiana* (2017, Kelsay Books) and *Coyotes I Couldn't See* (2016, Red Bird Chapbooks). He lives in Saint Paul, Minnesota.

Serena Jayne received her MFA in Writing Popular Fiction from Seton Hill University. Before becoming a writer, she worked as a research scientist, a fish stick slinger, a chat wrangler, and a race horse narc. When she isn't trolling art museums for works that move her, she enjoys writing in multiple fiction genres. Her short fiction and poetry has appeared in *Switchblade Magazine, Crack the Spine Literary Magazine, the Oddville Press* and other publications. www.serenajayne.com

Misha Burnett has little formal education, but has been writing poetry and fiction for around forty years. During this time he has supported himself and his family with a variety of jobs, including locksmith, cab driver, and building maintenance

John Timm writes short fiction in several genres. His work has appeared in *Bartleby Snopes, The Coffin Bell, Fiction Attics* and several anthologies. When not writing, John teaches Spanish and communication at a university in Phoenix, Arizona.

J.D. Graves is an author and playwright whose stage work has appeared at the New York International Fringe Festival and the FronteraFest. His short fiction can be found or is forthcoming in, *Switchblade #8, Mystery Weekly Magazine* Jan 2019, *Black Mask #4, Tough Crime #1, Broadswords and Blasters #6, Santa Cruz Weird*, etc. He is currently serving as the Editor-in-Chief of *EconoClash Review* and writing his first novel.

Alec Cizak is a writer from Indiana. His short stories have appeared in several journals and anthologies. His most recent novel, "Breaking Glass", is available from *ABC Group Documentation.* He is also the chief editor of the fiction journal *Pulp Modern.*

Robb T. White was born, raised, and still lives in Northeastern Ohio. He has published several crime, noir, and hardboiled novels. He's been nominated for a Derringer and many of his stories have appeared in magazines like *Yellow Mama, Black Cat Mystery Magazine, Switchblade,* and *Near to the Knuckle.* His new hardboiled series features private-eye Raimo Jarvi Northtown Eclipse (Fahrenheit Press, 2018). *Murder, Mayhem and More* cited "When You Run with Wolves" as one of the finalist for the Top Ten Crime books of 2018.

David Rachels is the author of "Verse Noir" (*Automat.Press*, 2017) and the editor of "Redheads Die Quickly and Other Stories": Expanded Edition by Gil Brewer (*Stark House Press,* 2019).

George Garnet's fiction has appeared or is forthcoming in a number of publications such as *Mystery Weekly, The Dark City Crime and Mystery Magazine, Switchblade, The Literary Hatchet, Heater, Needle in the Hay, The Lady in the Loft* and elsewhere. He lives in Melbourne.

Jim Wilsky is a crime fiction writer. He is the co-author, teamed with Frank Zafiro, of a four book series, published by *Down & Out Books;* "Blood on Blood", "Queen of Diamonds", "Closing the Circle" and "Harbinger". He also has a recently released book of short stories titled "Sort'em Out Later", also published by *Down & Out*. His short stories have appeared in some of the most respected online crime magazines and he has also contributed stories in several published anthologies, including *All Due Respect, Kwik Krimes, Both Barrels* and the soon to be released *The Odds Are Against Us.*

Special Thanks to cover models Jahnae, and Karla,*Creating Conversations Books*, The Switchblade L.A. Chapter, Rick West of *Battery Books*, Eric Beetner and S.W. Lauden of the

Writer Types podcast, for their continued support of *Switchblade*.